Joseph Ritson

Northern Garlands

A Collection of Songs

Joseph Ritson

Northern Garlands
A Collection of Songs

ISBN/EAN: 9783337008215

Printed in Europe, USA, Canada, Australia, Japan

Cover: Foto ©Andreas Hilbeck / pixelio.de

More available books at **www.hansebooks.com**

Northern Garlands.

" Books are both our luxuries and
our daily bread."

NORTHERN GARLANDS,

A COLLECTION OF SONGS

Edited by

JOSEPH RITSON.

(1784-1793.)

Edinburgh:
E. & G. GOLDSMID.
1887.

AD
ASTRA.

"*Inter Folia Fructus.*"

By Song "is anger forgotten, the Devil driven away, and melancholy and evil thoughts are expelled."

INTRODUCTION.

THE four small collections here reprinted have become extremely rare, and consequently no apologies are needed for their reproduction. The Volume contains—

1. The Bishopric Garland, or Durham Minstrel, which first appeared in 1784, and, again, enlarged in 1792.

2. The Yorkshire Garland, published in 1788.

3. The Northumberland Garland, dated 1793.

4. The North Country Chorister, issued in 1792.

The early editions were all very poorly printed. It is hoped that the present Volume will be found sufficiently artistic to please even the author of "Who Spoils our New English Books?"

THE

Bishopric Garland;

OR

DURHAM MINSTREL,

BEING A

CHOICE COLLECTION

OF

EXCELLENT SONGS

*Relating to the above County full of agreeable
variety and pleasant mirth.*

STOCKTON :
Printed by R. CHRISTOPHER.

MDCCLXXXIV.

Licensed and entered according to order.

Notice.

NUMBERS 1, 2, 6, 9, 15, and 16 of the following index were omitted in the edition of 1792, which at first only contained ten songs, but afterwards numbers 17 and 18, *not* in the first edition, were added.

CONTENTS.

—◦—§—◦—

		Page.
I.	The Durham Garland . .	17
II.	The Barnard Castle Tragedy	27
III.	Stockton's Commendation . .	32
IV.	A New Song in Praise of Stockton, for 1764	35
V.	The New Way of Stockton's Commendation	37
VI.	Stockton's Commendation (a New Song)	40
VII.	The Hare-Skin, by GEO. KNIGHT, Shoemaker . . .	43
VIII.	Limbo. By the same Authour .	47
IX.	The Launching of the Strickland. By the same . . .	50
X.	The Yorkshire Volunteers' Farewell to Stockton . . .	52
XI.	The Sedgfield Frolic .	56

XII. The Pleasures of Sunderland . 59

XIII. The Frolicsome Old Women of
Sunderland ; or, the Disappointed Young Maidens . . 61

XIV. A New Song made on Alice Marley 63

XV. A New Song in Praise of the
Durham Militia . . . 65

XVI. The Lass of Cockerton . . 68

XVII. Rookhope Ryde , . . . 70

XVIII. Lamentation on the Death of Sir
Robert de Nevill, Lord of Raby,
in 1282 79

THE
BISHOPRIC GARLAND,

OR

DURHAM MINSTREL.

SONG I.

The Durham Garland.

IN FOUR PARTS.

A Worthy lord of vast estate,
Who did in Durham dwell of late ;
But I will not declare his name,
By reason of his birth and fame.
But if you the truth would know,
This lord he did a hunting go,
He had indeed a noble train,
Of lords, and knights, and gentlemen.

Unto fam'd Yorkshire he would ride,
With all his gallants by his side.
In hunting pass'd the time away ;
But being weary, as they say,
His lordship lost his noble train,
Of lords, and knights, and gentlemen,
And hearing not the horns to blow,
He could not tell which way to go.

But he did wander to and fro,
Being weary, likewise full of woe :
At last, dame Fortune was so kind,
That he, the keeper's house did find.
He went and knocked at the gate,
And though it was so very late,
The forester he let him in,
And kindly entertained him.

But in the middle of the night,
When as the stars did shine so bright,
The lord was in a full surprise,
Being waked with a dismal noise.
Then did he rise, and call with speed,
To know the reason there indeed
Of all that shrieking and that noise,
Which did so much his soul surprise.

I'm sorry, Sir, the keeper said,
That you should be so much afraid,

But I hope that all will soon be well,
My wife is into labour fell.
This noble lord was learn'd and wise,
And knew the planets of the skies,
He saw an evil planet reign,
So call'd the forester again,

And gave him then to understand,
He'd have the midwife hold her hand :
But he was answer'd by the maid,
Her mistress was delivered :
At one o'Clock that very morn,
A lovely infant there was born :
He was indeed a pretty boy,
Which gave his parents mickle joy.

The lord was generous, kind and free,
And proffer'd Godfather to be.
This good man thank'd him heartily,
For his good will and curtesy.
A parson was call'd for with speed
For to christen the child indeed.
And after as we did hear say,
In joy and mirth they spent the day.

This noble lord did presents give,
And all the servants did receive,
He begg'd God would increase his store
For they had ne'er so much before

And likewise to the child he gave
A noble present, and a brave ;
It was a charming cabinet,
That was with pearls and rubies set.

Within a cabinet of gold,
Your eyes would dazzle to behold,
A richer gift, as I may say,
Has not been seen this many-a-day.
He charg'd his father faithfully
That he himself should keep the key,
Until the child could write and read
And then to give it him indeed.

Pray do not open it at all,
Whatever does to you befal,
For it may do my Godson good,
If it be rightly understood.
The second part it will unfold,
As true a tale as e'er was told,
Concerning of this lovely child,
Who was obedient, sweet, and mild.

PART II.

This child did take his learning so
If you the truth of this would know,
At eleven years of age indeed,
He could both Greek and Latin read.

But thinking of his cabinet,
Which was with pearls and jewels set,
He ask'd his father for the key,
The which he gave him speedily.

His cabinet he did unlock,
But he was in amazement struck,
When he the riches did behold,
And also saw the chain of Gold.
But searching farther he did find,
A paper that disturb'd his mind ;
Which was within the cabinet,
In Greek and Latin it was writ.

My son, serve God that is on high,
And pray to him incessantly,
Obey your parents, serve the king,
That nothing may your conscience sting.
For seven years hence your fate will be,
To be hanged upon a tree :
So pray to God, both night and day,
To let that hour pass away.

When he these rueful lines did read
He with a sigh did say, Indeed
If hanging be my destiny,
I'll from my friends and country flee :
For I will wander to and fro,
And go whither I do not know.

But first I'll ask my parents' leave,
In view their blessings to receive.

Then locking up the cabinet,
He went unto his chamber strait,
And went unto his parents dear,
Beseeching them with many a tear
That they would grant what he did crave
Your blessing first I beg to have,
And hope you'll let me go my way,
'Twill do me good another day.

For I indeed have made a vow,
But must not tell the reason now ;
But if I live I will return,
When seven years are pass'd and gone.
Both man and wife did then reply,
We fear, dear son, that you will die,
If we should yield to let you go,
Our aged hearts will burst with woe.

Yet he entreated eagerly,
So that they forc'd were to comply,
And gave consent that he should go,
But where, alas ! they did not know
In the third part you soon shall find,
That Fortune to him was most kind,
And after many dangers pass'd,
He came to Durham at the last.

PART III.

He went, by chance, as I've heard say,
Unto the house that very day,
Whereat his Godfather did dwell,
Now mind what fortune him befel.

This youth did crave a service there,
And strait came out the Godfather,
And seeing him a handsome youth,
He took him for his page in truth.
In this same place he pleas'd so well,
That above all he bore the bell,
And so well his lord did please,
He made him higher by degrees.

He made him butler indeed,
And then chief steward was with speed,
Which made the other servants spite,
And envy him, both day and night.
He ne'er was false in his trust,
But proved ever true and just,
And to the Lord did hourly pray,
To guard him still both night and day.

In this same place it doth appear,
He lived the space of seven years,
And oft his parents thought upon,
And of his promise to return.

Then humbly of his lord did crave,
That he his free consent might have,
For to go and see his parents dear,
Whom he had not seen for many years.

So having leave away he went
Not dreaming of the base intent
Which was contriv'd against him then,
By wicked, false, malicious men ;
Who had in his portmanteau put
Their noble lord's fine golden cup.
And when the lord at dinner was,
He miss'd the cup, as it came to pass.

Where should it be ? the lord did say,
We had it here but yesterday ;
The butler then reply'd with speed,
If you would know the truth indeed,
Your faithful Steward that is gone,
With feather'd nest away is flown ;
I do believe he has that and more,
Which does belong unto your store.

No, said the lord, that cannot be,
For I haue try'd his honesty ;
Then said the cook, my lord I'll die
Upon a tree that's nine feet high.
He hearing what this man did say,
Did send a messenger that day,

To take him with a hue and cry,
And bring him back immediately.

They search'd his portmanteau indeed,
In which they found the cup with speed,
Then he was struck with sad surprize,
And scarcely could believe his eyes ;
The lord then said unto him strait,
Thou shalt be hanged at my gate,
Because in you I put my trust,
And I took you for nought but just.

PART IV.

The day was fix'd, and being come
Said he, O Lord, it was my doom ;
Though innocent, I do declare
How my Lord's cup came to be there.
What fate decrees none can deny,
I was adjudged thus to die,
Upon a fatal gallows tree,
Which my Godfather did foresee.

In travailing pains my mother was,
Into the world I came at last,
A gentleman with skill did show,
Such death I now am coming to :
A chain and cabinet he gave
Unto my father, which I have,

The manuscript which was therein
Did show me plain I should be hang'd.

So the lord hearing him say so,
It came into his mind then to
Keep him from off the gallows high,
For I think this man is not guilty.
Something I doubt there is in this :
Methinks it is with mere malice
Of the cook and the butler too,
And if so, I'll make them rue.

The cause he tries a second time,
And found them guilty of the crime ;
They were adjudg'd to be hang'd strait,
Indeed they did deserve their fate.
The lord he took him, and did say,
Have you that cabinet, I pray ;
Yes, noble Lord, this is the same,
Was left me, with this very chain.

• My daughter is a virgin bright,
And you shall have her this very night ;
Wherefore now take delight in her,
'Tis I who am your Godfather.
Here's twenty thousand pounds in gold,
And when I'm dead it shall be told.
You shall enjoy my whole estate,
For to make you both rich and great.

SONG II.

THE BARNARDCASTLE TRAGEDY.

*Showing how one John Atkinson, of Murton near
Appleby, servant to Thomas Howson, miller,
at Barnardcastle, Bridge-end, courted the
said Howson's sister; and after he had gained
her entire affection by his wheedling solicita-
tions, left her disconsolate, and made courtship
to another, whom he married by the treacherous advice of one Thomas Skelton, who to save
the priest's fees, &c. performed the ceremony
himself; and upon her hearing the news,
broke her heart, and bled to death on the spot.
This being both true and tragical, 'tis hoped
'twill be a warning to all lovers.*

Tune of *Constant Anthony.*

YOUNG men and maidens all, I pray you now
attend,
Mark well this tragedy which you find here penn'd,
At Barnardcastle Bridge-end, an honest man lives
there,
His calling grinding corn, for which few can
compare.

He had a sister dear, in whom he took delight,
And Atkinson, his man, woo'd her both day and
    night,
Till thro' process of time he chain'd fast her heart,
Which prov'd her overthrow, by Death's surpris-
    ing dart.

False-hearted Atkinson, with his deluding tongue,
And his fair promises, he's this poor maid undone;
For when he found he'd caught her fast in Cupid's
    snare,
Then made he all alike, Betty's no more his dear

Drinking was his delight, his senses to doze,
Keeping lewd company, when he should repose;
His money being spent, and they would tick no
    score,
Then with a face of brass, he ask'd poor Betty
    more.

He at length met with one, a serving-maid in town
Who for good ale and beer often would pawn her
    gown,
And at all-fours she'd play, as many people know,
A fairer gamester no man could ever show.

Tom Skelton, ostler at the King's-arms does dwell,
Who this false Atkinson did all his secrets tell;
He let him understand of a new love he'd got,
And with an oath he swore, she'd keep full the pot.

Then for the girl they sent, Betty Hardy was her
    name,
Who to her mistress soon an excuse did frame ;
Mistress, I have a friend at the King's-arms doth
    stay,
Which I desire to see, before he go away.

Then she goes to her friend, who she finds ready
    there,
Who catch'd her in his arms, how does my only
    dear,
She says, Boys drink about, and fear no reckonings
    large,
For she had pawn'd her smock, to defray the
    charge.

They did carouse it off, till they began to warm,
Says Skelton make a match, I pray where's the
    harm ?
Then with a loving kiss they straightway did
    agree,
But they no money had, to give the priest a fee.

Quoth Skelton seriously, the priest's fee is large,
I'll marry you myself, and save you all the charge ;
Then they plight their troth unto each other there,
Went two miles from the town, and goes to bed
    we hear.

Then when the morning came, by breaking of the
    day,
He had some corn to grind, he could no longer
    stay ;
My business is in haste, which I to thee do tell,
So took a gentle kiss, and bid his love farewell.

Now, when he was come home, and at his busi-
    ness there,
His master's sister came, who was his former dear ;
Betty, he said, I'm wed, certainly I protest,
Then she smil'd in his face, sure you do but Jest.

Then within few days space, his wife unto him
    went,
And to the sign o' th' Last, there she for him sent,
The people of the house finding what was in hand,
Stept out immediately, let Betty understand.

Now this surprising news caus'd her fall in a trance,
Life as she was dead, no limbs she could advance,
Then her dear brother came, her from the ground
    he took
And she spake up and said, O my poor heart is
    broke.

Then with all speed they went, for to undo her lace,
Whilst at her nose and mouth her heart's blood
    ran apace.

Some stood half dead by her, others for help
    inquire,
But in a moment's time, her life it did expire.

    False hearted lovers all, let this a warning be,
    For it may well be called Betty Howson's
        Tragedy.

SONG III.

Stockton's Commendation.

AN OLD SONG.

To the Tune of *Sir John Fenwick's the flower among them.*

Come brave spirits, that love Canary,
  And good company are keeping,
From our friends let's never vary,
  Let your muse awake from sleeping.
Bring forth mirth and wise Apollo;
  Mark your eyes on a true relation:
Virgil, with his pen, shall follow,
  In ancient Stockton's commendation.

Upon the stately river Tees,
  A goodly castle there was placed,
Nigh joining to the ocean seas,
  Whereby our country was much graced
Affording rich commodities,
  With corn and lead unto our nation;
Which makes me sing with cheerful voice,
Of ancient Stockton's commendation.

In sixteen hundred thirty-five,
  And about the month of February,
Three Stockton-men they did contrive,
  To see their friends, and to be merry :
Part of their names I shall describe,
  And place them down in comely fashion,
There was William, John, and Anthony,
  Gain'd ancient Stockton commendation.

To famous Richmond first they came,
  And with their friends a while remained,
Middleham there, that town of fame,
  Whereby much credit they obtained :
Being merry on a day,
  A challenge came in this same fashion,
A match at foot-ball for to play ;
  But Stockton got the commendation.

Three Middleham-men appointed were,
  And stakes put down on either party ;
Stockton-men cast off all fear,
  For Bishopric was always hearty :
Then those three Middleham-men did yield,
  And for their loss they seem'd to murmur ;
There was but one came to the field,
  The other two at home remained.

With shouts and cries, in cheerful wise,
  The country all about them dwelling,
                C

They did say that very day,
  That Stockton-men were far excelling.
When first I did it understand,
  It was told to me as a true relation,
Then I took my pen and ink in hand,
  And I writ brave Stockton's commendation

ᴀ ɴᴇᴡ ꜱᴏɴɢ

IN PRAISE OF STOCKTON, FOR THE YEAR 1764.

BY MR. WILLIAM SUTTON.

On the banks of the Tees, at Stockton of old,
A Castle there was of great fame we are told,
Where the bishops of Durham were wont to
retreat,
And spend all their summers at that gallant seat.
Derry Down, &c.

'Twas once on a time, that King John being there,
The chiefs of Newcastle did thither repair ;
Humbly pray'd that his Highness would deign for
to grant
Them a charter, of which they were then in great
want.

The King highly pleas'd with the Bishop's grand
treat,
Abounding in liquors, and all sorts of meat,
Their prayer comply'd with, the charter did sign,
Owing then, as 'twas said, to the Bishop's good
wine.

Old Noll, in his day, out of pious concern,
This castle demolish'd, sold all but the barn,
When Nilthorp and Hollis, with two or three
    more
Divided the spoils, as they'd oft done before.

The town still improving became the delight
Of strangers and others, so charming its sight ;
That a Bridge cross the river being lately pro-
    pos'd,
The cash was subscribed, and the bargain soon
    clos'd.

The King, Lords, and Commons approving the
    scheme,
The bridge was begun, and now's building between
Two counties, when finish'd no doubt 'twill pro-
    duce,
Fairs, markets for cattle, and all things for use.

Let us drink then a bumper to Stockton's success;
May its commerce increasing ne'er meet with dis-
    tress ;
May the people's endeavours procure them much
    wealth,
And enjoy all their days the great blessing of
    health.

                              Derry Down, &c.

SONG V.

THE NEW WAY OF

Stockton's Commendation.

To the old Tune.

BY BENJAMIN PYE, LL.D.

ARCHDEACON OF DURHAM.

" Upon the stately river Tees,
    " A noble castle there was placed,
" Nigh unto the ocean seas,
    " Whereby our country was much graced :
" Affording rich commodities,
    " Of corn and lead unto the nation ;
" Which makes me sing in a cheerful wise,
    " Of ancient Stockton's commendation.

But now I'll tell you news prodigious,
    My honest friends be sure remark it,
Our ferries are transform'd to bridges,
    And Cleveland trips to Stockton market.
Our causeways rough, and miry roads,
    Shall sink into a navigation,

And Johnny Carr shall sing fine odes,
   In modern Stockton's commendation.

O what a scene for joy and laughter,
   To see, as light as cork or feather,
Our ponderous lead and bulky rafter,
   Sail down the smooth canal together.
Whilst coal and lime, and cheese and butter,
   Shall grace our famous navigation,
And we will make a wondrous clutter,
   In modern Stockton's commendation.

Our fairs I will next celebrate,
   With scores of graziers, hinds and jockeys;
And bumpkins yok'd with Nell and Kate,
   Who stare like any pig that stuck is:
Fat horned beasts now line our streets,
   Which Aldermen were wont to pace on;
And oxen low, and lambkins bleat,
   And all for Stockton's commendation.

Our races too deserve a tune,
   The Northern sportsmen all prefer 'em,
For Dainty Davy here did run
   Much better than at York or Durham.
O 'twould take up a swingeing volume,
   To sing at large our reputation,
Our bridge, our shambles, cross and column,
   All speak fair Stockton's commendation.

Fill then your jovial bumpers round,
   Join chorus all in Stockton's glory,
Let us but love our native town,
   A fig for patriot, whig, or tory
Whate'er they say, whate'er they do,
   Their aim is but to fleece the nation ;
Let us continue firm and true,
     To honest Stockton's commendation.

Stockton's Commendation.

A NEW SONG.

YE freeholders of Stockton-town,
Who follow your several occupations,
Once more I'll sing, and raise my tune,
On flourishing Stockton's commendations.

Our bridge with pleasure I behold,
Our shambles gain great approbation,
And neigh'bring towns agree with me,
In singing Stockton's commendation.

From East and West the graziers bring
Fat flocks of each denomination ;
And o'er a glass they freely sing
Great is Stockton's commendation.

Full thirty miles some butchers ride ;
Fat goods are their expectation,
At Stockton they are well supplied,
They sing Stockton's commendation.

Our shows proclaim a thriving town,
And fortnight-days to admiration,
To see Stockton improve so soon,
Daily to her commendation.

Our spacious streets each stranger views,
And fairly gives his approbation,
Stockton's the place that I do choose,
So great is Stockton's commendation.

Our gardens, orchards, river, plains,
All join to raise our contemplation,
While hand in hand we other join,
In singing Stockton's commendation.

Our merchants cast a noble shew,
Rich goods as any in the nation,
Great is their trade with high and low,
Makes them sing Stockton's commendation.

All trades shall flourish now I see,
In their several occupation :
And all our song it shall be,
Stockton's lasting commendation.

Our ship's well stor'd with merchandize,
And all do keep their proper station :
Our neighb'ring towns with good supply,
Makes them sing Stockton's commendation.

Our wool-trade daily does increase,
The staple of the British nation :
And farmers come, with cheerful pace,
To join in Stockton's commendation.

Our lead in piles in plenty lie,
Sent by shipping to each nation.
Behold all trades on Stockton smile,
Makes me sing Stockton's commendation.

Our races they are fifties three,
Where Darlington, of noble station,
Our Steward he approves to be,
To honour Stockton's commendation.

May Darlington be Stockton's friend,
And Stockton give their approbation
In favour of the House of Vane,
For raising Stockton's commendation.

Now, Freeholders, I take my leave,
Success to the British nation,
These lines to you I freely give,
In praise of Stockton's commendation.

SONG VII.

THE HARE-SKIN.

BY GEORGE KNIGHT, SHOEMAKER.

Tune—Have you heard of a frolicsome ditty ?

COME, gentlemen attend to my ditty,
    All you that delight in a gun ;
And if you'll be silent a minute,
    I'll tell you a rare piece of fun.
                    Fal lal, &c.

It was on the tenth of November,
    Or else upon Martinmas-day,
A gentleman who loved pastime,
    He got a hare-skin stuff'd with hay.

Then into the fields he convey'd her,
    And set her against a hedge-side ;
Our gunners were rambling the fields,
    So that pussy was quickly espy'd.

Mr. Tindal was the first that espy'd her ;
    He said that he lov'd roast hare,
And that he would have her *tit* supper,
    For he for the law did not care.

The better for to complete it,
  He charged his gun well with slugs,
With that he let fly at her,
  And *hat* her betwixt the two lugs.

But when that he went for to seize her,
  He found he was depriv'd of his bit ;
He flung her down in a passion,
  And look'd as if he'd been b——t.

The next was Will Dunn, our painter,
  Who wanted a novelty-bit ;
And then he let fly at her,
  And kill'd her stone dead on her seat.

When firing he swore he had maul'd her
  He never missed a hare in his life ;
And then in great trouble was he,
  For to get her safe home to his wife.

The next was John Walker, a tailor,
  He thinking poor Puss for to knap ;
Indeed he endeavour'd to kill her,
  But his gun very often did snap.

But then making all things in good order,
  Then at her he did let drive,
And our serjeant was to have her *tit* supper,
  To make them all merry belyve.

But I think he was damnable saucy,
  For she wasn't meat for such as he ;
He must get something else to his cabbage,
  For it and hare-flesh 'll ne'er agree.

The next was Joe our barber,
  One morning he rose in great haste,
And swore he would have a hare *tiv* his
    supper,
  And give all his neighbours a taste.

When firing, he swore he had kill'd her,
  O then in great trouble was he,
How that he might safely convey her,
  For fear any body should see.

The next was John Blythman, Esquire,
  Indeed, he was much to blame
To kill a hare with his gun, it shouldn't be
    done,
  For it spoils all a gentleman's game.

Then Grundy came cursing and swearing,
  Which is the chief end of his talk,
He shot her, and swore by his Maker,
  He'd kill'd her as dead as a mawk.

But when that he went for to seize her,
  And found it a skin stuff'd with hay,

He flung her down in a passion,
  And cursed, and so went away.

Now I would have you all to take care for the
    future,
  And mind very well what I say,
When you fire your gun, pray ye see the hare run,
  Lest it prove a hare-skin stuff'd with hay.

But I think they were all finely tricked,
  Beside wasting their powder and shot;
Let us have a good drink at the fancy
  So, Landlady fill us the pot.

Here's the gentleman's health that contriv'd it,
  For he is a right honest soul;
We'll laugh and we'll merrily sing,
  When we're over a full flowing bowl.
                              Fal, lal, &c.

SONG VIII.

LIMBO.

BY THE SAME AUTHOR.

Tune, *On a time I was great, now little I'm grown.*

I'LL tell you a story, if you please to attend,
    When my heart was afflicted with sorrow,
This song it is new, but it's absolute true ;
    It's for nothing I did buy or borrow :
But I was sent for to Preston's, one day the last
    week,
There I little expected with what I did meet,
But the country's all rogues, and the world is a
    cheat,
    And there they confined me in Limbo.

Like an innocent lamb to the slaughter I went,
    Not knowing what was their intention,
But when I came there, O how I did stare,
    When I found out their damned invention.
There was Preston the bailiff, Joseph Craggs was
    his bum,
And there they did seize me as sure as a gun,
Upstairs then they haul me into the back room,
    And there they confin'd me in Limbo.

My belly was empty, though my stomach was full,
  For to think there how I was *trapanded*,
Preston pull'd out a paper, and he made a long
  scrawl,
  And he forc't me for to set my hand to't.
Then I open'd his closet, and got out a pie,
Then I call'd for liquor, while I was a-dry,
I knew somebody would pay for it, but what
  cared I?
  I wasn't to starve, though in Limbo.

Another poor fellow there happen'd to be,
  Which they had confined in Limbo ;
Brother-prisoner, says I, how shall we get free,
  For want of this thing called rhino?
The poor fellow sat like one was half dead,
Then I gave him claret to dye his nose red ;
But I never knew yet how the reckoning was paid:
  I was resolv'd to live well though in Limbo.

There was Mr. Bum and I, we toss'd it about,
  Until we began to grow mellow ;
Three bottles of claret he there did me give,
  Indeed he's a jolly good fellow.
Full bumpers of claret went round it is true,
Some drank for vexation till twice they did spew,
But ne'er in my life I saw such a merry crew,
  As we were when I was in Limbo.

There was Ralph Jackson, the tanner, he came in
    by chance,
  And did chatter and talk like a parrot ;
And likewise Will Bulmer was one of our number,
    For he had a mind to drink claret.
Full glasses went round, till I could not see,
O then they were all willing that I should go free;
But the devil may pay their reckoning for me,
    For now I have got out of Limbo.

With many a foul step I stagger'd home at last,
    And it happened to be without falling ;
I got on my bed, and nothing I said,
    But my wife she began with her bawling ;
She rung me such a peal, though she'd been not
    well,
As if she would have rais'd all the devils in hell,
You might have heard her as far as the sound of
    Bow-bell,
    Then I wish'd that I'd stay'd there in Limbo.

The Launching of the Strickland.

BY THE SAME.

Tune, *Robin Hood and the Tanner*.

GOOD people draw near, and I'll let you hear,
　　With a hey down, down and a dee,
What happen'd the other day,
It was on twelfth-eve, if you will me believe,
　　The people came flocking this way.

When I squeez'd along in the thick of the throng,
　　I *see* men a splitting of blocks ;
O I knew what they meant ; it was their intent
　　For to launch a ship off o' the stocks.

There I *see Mother's Lull*, O a bottle he had full,
　　I suppose't to be very good wine ;
They booz'd it about, till it was almost out,
　　It's customar' at such a time.

Frank stood on his guard, ready to discharge
　　The bottle he held in his hand
He was to call her the *Strickland*, but he had
　　　been tipling,
　　For he was scarce able to stand.

Howsomever, Blue and Black, he stood to his tack,
 And just as the ship was a starting,
The bottle he threw, indeed it is true,
 But he miss'd the ship, and *hat* the captain.

O he *hat* him on the breast, I vow and protest,
 I wouldn't have been in his place;
He did him surprise, he might ha' drove out his
  eyes,
 If the bottle had hit in his face.

So God bless the king, this joke we will sing
 On Saturday-night when we're tipling
We'll drink to our wives, the captain, men and
  boys,
 And all that belong to the *Strickland*.

SONG X.

HARK TO WINCHESTER.

*or, the Yorkshire Volunteer's farewell to
the good folks of Stockton.*

Tune, *Push about the Jorum.*

YE Stockton lads and lasses too,
  Come listen to my story,
A dismal tale, because 'tis true,
  I've now to lay before ye:
We must away, our rout is come
  We scarce refrain from tears, O:
Shrill shrieks the fife, rough roars the drum,—
  March Yorkshire Volunteers, O!
                    Fal lal lal la ral.

Yet ere we part, my comrades say,
  Come, Stockhore,* you're the poe
If e're you'd pen a greatful lay,
  'Tis now the time to show it.

---

* Herbert Stockhore, a private, the pretended author.

Such usage fair in this good town,
   We've met from age and youth, Sirs.
Accept our grateful thanks and own,
   A poet sings the truth, Sirs.
                   Fal lal, &c.

Ye lasses too, of all I see,
   The fairest in the nation ;
Sweet buds of beauty's blooming tree,
   The top of the creation ;
Full many of our lads I ween,
   Have good good wives and true, Sirs,
I wonder what our leaders mean,
   They have not done so too, Sirs.
                   Fal lal, &c.

Perhaps—but hark ! the thund'ring drum,
   From love to arms is beating ;
Our country calls ; we come, we come,
   Great George's praise repeating ;
He's great and good, long may he here
   Reign, every bliss possessing ;
And long may each true volunteer
   Behold him Britain's blessing.
                   Fal lal, &c.

Our valiant Earl shall lead us on
   The nearest way to glory,

Bright Honour hails her darling son,
  And Fame records his story :
Dundas commands upon our lists
  The second, tho' on earth, Sirs,
No one he's second to exists,
  For courage, sense, and worth, Sirs.
                    Fal lal, &c.

No venal muse before your view
  Next sets a veteran bold, Sirs,
The praise to merit justly due,
  From Paul she cannot hold, Sirs ;
His valour oft has bore the test,
  In war he's brisk and handy,
His private virtues stand confest,
  In short, he's quite the dandy.
                    Fal lal, &c.

Brave Mackarel heads his grenadiers,
  They're just the lads to do it,
And should the Dons, or lank Monsieurs
  Come here he'll make them rue it,
He'll roar his thunders, make them flee,
  With a tow, row, row, row, ra, ra ;
And do them o'er by land,—at sea
  As Rodney did Langara.
                    Fal lal, &c.

Young Thompson with his lads so light
  Of foot, with hearts of steel, O

His country's cause will nobly fight,
    And make her foes to feel, O,
For should the frog-fed sons of Gaul
    Come capering, *a la François,*
My lads, said he, we'll teach them all
    The *Light Bob* country-dance, a.
                    Fal lal, &c.

Our leaders all, so brave, and bold,
    Should in verse, recite a,
A baggage waggon would not hold
    The songs that I could write, a,
Their deeds so great, their words so mild,
    O take our worst commander,
And to him Cæsar was a child
    And so was Alexander.
                    Fal lal, &c.

Such men as these we'll follow thro'
    The world, and brave all danger,
Each volunteer is firm and true,
    His heart's to fear a stranger.—
Good Folks, farewell! God bless the King
    With angels centry o'er him
Now, *Hark to Winchester!* we'll sing
    And push about the Jorum !
                    Fal lal lal la ral.

The Sedgfield Frolic.

COME all ye gallant brave wenches,
   That love strong liquor so well,
And use to fuddle your noses,
   Come listen to what I shall tell :
Your praises abroad I will thunder,
   'Tis pity you should go free,
And the wanton lasses of Sedgfield
   Are roaring company.

Come, Landlady, fill us a bumper,
   And take no thought for the shot,
It is a sin as I hope to be saved,
   To part with an empty pot ;
Let the glass go merrily round,
   Our business is jolly to be,·
And the wanton lasses of Sedgfield
   Are roaring company.

Who are they that dare oppose us,
   Since we are together met?
We will tipple and fuddle our noses,
   Our frolic to complete ;

For our frolic it is begun,
  And we will end it merrily,
And the ranting lasses of Sedgfield
  Are roaring company.

There's Middleton as brisk as a bottle,
  She merrily leads the van,
And Crispe, the butcher's daughter,
  She'll follow as fast as she can.
There's the sempstress and her sister
  The rear drive merrily,
And the ranting lasses of Sedgfield
  Are roaring company.

Each one shall take her quantum,
  Thus says brave Middleton ;
We will drink a health to Peg Trantum,
  And merrily we'll go on ;
Let the shot be never so great,
  I'll speak to my landlady ;
And the ranting lasses of Sedgfield
  Are roaring company.

There's a brave sinking tailor,
  That hath a brisk handsome wife,
And she will convey the flaggon,
  To avoid all future strife :
And the baker, at the next door,
  She will be the landlady ;

And the ranting lasses of Sedgfield
  Are roaring company.

There's Branson, an honest fellow,
  He hath sugar enough in store,
If cloves and mace be wanting,
  We will boldly run on the score :
For our wanton frolic is begun,
  And we'll end it most merrily,
And the wanton lasses of Sedgfield
  Are roaring company.

Two wives I had almost forgotten,
  Which I must touch in the quick,
Being merry at Mr. Branson's,
  They danc'd 'bout the candlestick,
And the tune was juice of Barley,
  Which made them dance merrily,
And long did they hold a parley,
  And made jolly company.

In the midst of this great pother,
  The backish wife came in,
She was forced to be led by another.
  Thro' thick and likewise thro' thin.
And thus they did end their frolic,
  Good fellow I'll tell to thee,
And the ranting lasses of Sedgfield
  Are roaring company.

SONG XII.

The Pleasures of Sunderland.

In the fine town of Sunderland, which stands on
a hill,
Which stands on a hill most noble to see,
There's fishing and fowling all in the same town,
Every man to his mind, but Sunderland for me.

There's dancing and singing also in the town,
And many hot scolds there are in the week;
'Tis pleasant indeed the market to see,
And the young maids that are mild and meek.

The damsels of Sunderland would, if they could,
To welcome brave sailors, when they come
from sea,
Build a fine tower of silver and gold;
Every man to his mind, but Sunderland for me.

The young men of Sunderland are pretty blades,
And when they come in with these handsome
maids,
They kiss and embrace, and compliment free;
Every man to his mind, but Sunderland for me.

In silver-street there lives one Isabel Rod
  She steeps the best ale the town can afford
For gentlemen to drink till they cannot see
  Every man to his mind, but Sunderland for me.

Sunderland's a fine place, it shines where it stands,
  And the more I look on it the more my heart
    warms;
And if I was there I would make myself free:
  Every man to his mind, but Sunderland for me.

SONG XIII.

The frolicsome Old Women of Sunderland,

OR, THE DISAPPOINTED YOUNG MAIDS.

To the Tune of, *They'll marry, tho' threescore and ten.*

You Sunderland lasses draw near,
Sure you are forsaken by men
    But the old women, they
    Forget for to play
But will get married at threescore and ten.

You Sunderland lasses are slow,
And yet there's good choice of young men ;
    The old women, they
    Do shew you fair play,
They get married at threescore and ten.

A house that's within full sea mark,
Is very well accustomed by men ;
    But better had they
    To live honest, I say,
Or get married at threescore and ten.

There are sailors that are clever young blades,
And keel-bullies like unto them,
    You maids that are fair,
    Get married this year,
Lest you tarry till threescore and ten.

The old women carry the day
They beat both the maids and the men
    To give Sunderland the sway,
    For ever and ay,
They'll marry tho' threescore and ten.

SONG XIV.

A NEW SONG

Made on Alice Marley.

AN ALEWIFE, AT *****, NEAR CHESTER.

ELSIE* Marley is grown so fine,
She wont get up to serve her swine,
But lies in bed till eight or nine,
And surely she does take her time.
    And do you ken Elsie Marley, honey?
    The wife who sells the barley, honey;
    She wont get up to serve her swine,
    And do you ken Elsie Marley, honey?

Elsie Marley is so neat,
It is hard for one to walk the street,
But every lad and lass they meet,
Cries do you ken Elsie Marley, honey?

Elsie keeps wine, gin, and ale,
In her house below the dale.
Where every tradesman up and down,
Does call and spend his half-a-crown.

---

* Elsie altered throughout to Alice *second edit.*

The farmers as they come that way,
They drink with Elsie every day,
And call the fiddler for to play
The tune of Elsie Marley, honey.

The pitmen and the keelmen trim,
They drink bumbo made of gin
And for to dance they do begin
The tune of Elsie Marley, honey.

The sailors they will call for flip,
As soon as they come from the ship,
And then begin to dance and skip,
To the tune of Elsie Marley, honey.

Those gentlemen that go so fine,
They'll treat her with a bottle of wine,
And freely they'll sit down and dine
Along with Elsie Marley, honey.

So to conclude these lines I've penn'd
Hoping there's none I do offend
And thus my merry joke doth end
Concerning Elsie Marley, honey.

SONG XV.

A NEW SONG,

In Praise of the Durham Militia.

Tune, *The Lilies of France.*

MILITIA boys for my theme I now chuse,
(Your aid I implore to assist me, my muse),
Whilst I relate of the Durham youth's fame,
Who cheerful appear'd when these new tidings
    came,
That to Barnardcastle they must march away,
Embody'd to be, without stop or delay.

What tho' some cowards have betook them to
    flight,
And for their king and country scorn for to fight,
Yet we Durham boys, who jovial appear,
Right honest we'll be, and we'll banish all fear,
When head of the front, how martial we see
Our Colonel so brave, so gallant and free.

Whose generous heart, by experience we know,
Why need we then dread along with him to go?
Then farewell, dear wives, and each kind sweet-
    heart,
Pray do not repine that from you we must part ;
But, hark ! the drums beat, and the fifes sweetly
    play,
We're order'd to march now to Richmond straight
    way.

Where, cloathed in red, and in purple attire,
Our exercise then shall be all our desire,
Which having acquir'd, then we'll merrily sing,
Success to great George, and the Prussian king,
Likewise loyal Pitt, a statesman so bold,
Who scorns to be false, for interest or gold.

If then the Monsieurs should with their crafty
    guile,
E'er dare to molest us on Britain's fair isle,
We'll laugh at their fury, and malice so strong,
To Charon below how we'll hurl them headlong.
Do they think that our muskets useless shall be,
When in numbers great them advancing we see.

If they do, they're mista'en, we'll boldly proceed ;
And conquer or die, ere ignobly we'll yield :
Then crowned with laurel, (for vent'ring our lives)
Home then we'll return to our sweethearts and
    wies,

What joy will be greater, our fame shall abound,
The bells then shall ring, and the trumpets shall
    sound.

Let each loyal Briton fill up his glass,
For to drive care away, so round let it pass,
Drink a health to king George, who sits on his
    throne,
(Whose power the French to their sorrow have
    known),
May the heavens above preserve him from harm,
And ever defend him from foreign alarms.

SONG XVI.

The Lass of Cockerton.

Tune, *Low down in the Broom.*

'TWAS on a summer's evening,
  As I a roving vent,
I met a maiden fresh and fair,
  That was a milking sent.
Whose lovely look such sweetness spoke,
  Divinely fair she shone ;
With modest face her dwelling-place,
  I found was Cockerton.

With raptures fir'd, I eager gazd,
  On this blooming country maid,
My roving eye, in quickest search,
  Each graceful charm survey'd.
The more I gaz'd, a new wonder rais'd,
  And still I thought upon
Those lovely charms, that so alarms
  In the Lass of Cockerton.

Now would the Gods but deign to hear
   An artless lover's prayer ;
This lovely nymph I'd ask,
   And scorn each other care.
True happiness I'd then possess,
   Her love to share alone ;
No mortals know what pleasures flow,
   With the Lass of Cockerton.

SONG XVII.

ROOKHOPE-RYDE.*

A Bishoprick border-song, composed in 1569;
taken down from the chanting of George
Collingwood the elder, late of Boltsburn, in the
neighbourhood of Ryhope, who was intered at
Stanhope the 16th December 1785; never
before printed.

> ROOKHOPE stands in a pleasant place,
> If the false thieves wad let it be
> But away they steal our goods apace
> And ever an ill death may they die !†

---

* *Rookhope* is the name of a valley about five miles
in length, at the termination of which *Rookhope-burn*
empties itself into the river Wear, and is the north
part of the parish of Stanhope in Weardale. *Rookhope-
head* is the top of the vale. *Ryde* is an *inroad*, or, as
the Scots call it, a *raid*.

†So, in a ballad of "Northumberland betrayed by
Douglas," printed in Percy's *Reliques*, i. 233:

"And ever an ill death may they die."

And so is the man of Thirlwa' 'nd Willie-havei,*
And all their companies thereabout,
That is minded to do mischief,
And as their stealing stands not out.

But yet we will not slander them all,
For there is of them good enough ;
It is a sore consumed tree
That on it bears not one fresh bough.

Lord God ! is not this a pitiful case,
That men dare not drive their goods to t' feil,
But limmer thieves drives them away,
That fears neither heaven nor hell.

---

* *Thirlwall* or *Thirlitwall* is said by Fordun, the
Scottish historian, to be a name given to the Pictish or
Roman wall, from its having been *thirled*, or *perforated*,
in ancient times, by the Scots and Picts. Wyntown,
also, who, most probably, copied Fordun, calls it
Thirlwall. Thirlwall-castle, though in a very ruinous
condition, is still standing by the side of this famous
wall, upon the river Tippal. It gave name to the
ancient family, *de-Thirlwall. Willie-haver*, or *Willeva*,
is a small district or township in the parish of
Lanercost, near Bewcastle-dale in Cumberland ; mentioned in the old border-ballad of *Hobie Noble* :

" Go war the bows of Hartlie-burn
  See they sharp their arrows on the wa' :
Warn *Willeva*, and spear Edom
  And see the morn they meet me a'."

Lord, send us peace into the realm,
  That every man may live on his own !
I trust to God, if it be his will,
  That Weardale-men may never be overthrown,

For great troubles they've had in hand
  With borderers pricking hither and thither,
But the greatest fray that e'er they had
  Was with the 'men' of Thirlwa' 'nd Williehaver.

They gather'd together so royally,
  The stoutest men and the best in gear ;
And he that rade not on a horse,
  I wat he rade on a weil-fed mear.

So in the morning before they came out,
  So well I wot they broke their fast,
In the [forenoon they came] unto a bye fell,
  Where some of them did eat their last.*

When they had eaten aye and done,
  They say'd, some captains here needs must be :
Then they choose'd forth Harry Corbyl,
  And ' Symon Fell,' and Martin Ridley.

Then o'er the moss, where as they came,
  With many a brank and whew,
One of them could to another say,
  I think this day we are men enew.

---

* This would be about eleven o'clock, the usual
dinner hour at that period.

For Weardale-men is a journey ta'en,
   They are so far out o'er yon fell,
That some of them's with the two earls
   And others fast in Barnard-castell.*

There we shall get gear enough,
   For there is nane but women at hame,
The sorrowful fend that they can make,
   Is loudly cries † as they were slain.

Then in at Rookhope-head they came,
   And there they thought tul a' had their prey,

---

* The two earls were Thomas Percy, earl of
Northumberland and Charles Nevil, earl of Westmoreland, who, on the 15th November, 1569, at the head
of their tenantry and others, took arms for the pur-
pose of liberating Mary queen of Scots, and restoring
the old religion. They besieged Barnard-castle, which
was, for eleven days, stoutly defended by sir George
Bowes, who, afterward, being appointed the queen's
marshal, hanged the poor constables and peasantry by
dozens in a day, to the amount of 800. The earl of
Northumberland, betrayed by the Scots, with whom
he had taken refuge, was beheaded at York, on the
22d of August, 1572, and the earl of Westmoreland
deprived of the ancient and noble patrimony of the
Nevils, and reduced to beggary, escaped over sea, into
Flanders and died in misery and disgrace, being the
last of his family. See two ballads on this subject, in
Percy's collection (I, 271, 281), and consider whe'her
they be genuine.

† This is still the phraseology of Westmoreland : a
poorly man, a *softly* day, and the like.

They were number'd to never a man
  But forty under fifty.

The thieves was number'd a hundred men
  I wat they were not of the worst,
That could be choose'd out of Thirlwa' 'nd Willie-
    haver
  [I trow they were the very first]. *

But all that was in Rookhope-head,
  And all that was i' Nuketon-cleugh,
Where Weardale-men o'ertook the thieves,
  And there they gave them fighting eneugh.

So sore they made them fain to flee,
  As many was ' a " out of hand,
And, for tul have been at home again,
  They would have been in iron bands :

And for the space of long seven years
  As sore they mighten a' had their lives
But there was never one of them
  That ever thought to have seen their ' wives.'

About the time the fray began
  I trow it lasted but an hour
Till many a man lay weaponless
  And was sore wounded in that stour.

---

*The reciter, from his advanced age, could not
recollect the original line thus imperfectly supplied.

Also before that hour was done,
  Four of the thieves were slain,
Besides all those that wounded were,
  And eleven prisoners there was ta'en.

George Carrick and his brother Edie,
  Them two, I wot, they were both slain ;
Harry Corbyl, and Lennie Carrick,
  Bore them company in their pain.

One of our Weardale-men was slain,
  Rowland Emerson his name hight ;
I trust to God his soul is well,
  Because he ' fought' unto the right.

But thus they say'd, We'll not depart
  While we have one :—Speed back again !
And when they came amongst the dead men,
  There they found George Carrick slain.

And when they found George Carrick slain,
  I wot it went well near their ' heart,'
Lord let them never make a better end,
  That comes to play them sicken a 'part.'

I trust to God no more they shal,
  Except it be one for a great chance ;
For God wil punish all those
  With a great heavy pestilence.

Thir limmer thieves, they have good hearts,
   They never think to be o'erthrown,
Three banners against Weardale-men they bare,
   As if the world had been all their own.

Thir Weardale-men they have good hearts,
   They are as ſtiſ as any tree,
For, if they'd every one been slain,
   Never a ſoot back man would flee.

And such a storm amongst them ſell,
   As I think you never heard the like ;
For he that bears his head so high,
   He oſt-times ſalls into the dyke.

And now i do entreat you all,
   As many as are present here,
To pray for singer of this song,
   For he sings to make blithe your cheer.

SONG XIV.

LAMENTATION.

On the death of sir ROBERT DE NEVILI., Lord of
Raby, in 1282; alluding to an ancient custom,
of offering a stag at the high altar of Durham-
abbey on Holy-rood-day, accompanyed with the
winding of horns.

> WEL-I-WA, sal ys hornes blaw,
> Holy-rode this day;
> Nou es he dede, and lies law,
> Was wont to blaw them ay.
>
> .   .   .   .

NOTES.

PAGE 32.—STOCKTON'S COMMENDATION.

Bell, in his *Rhymes of Northern Bards*, says :—
"During the scarcity of change in 1811-12, the
people of Stockton issued out silver tokens of
sixpence and twelvepence value, the only tokens
issued in the county."

PAGE 58.—SEDGEFIELD FROLIC.

Bell gives "Juice of the Barley," in italics.

PAGE 63.—ELSIE MARLEY.

* * * * * is Picktree, near Chester-le-street.

PAGE 68.—THE LASS OF COCKERTON.

Cockerton is a village near Darlington.

APPENDIX.

THE two following songs will prove interesting
to the reader, though they do not form part of
Ritson's Collection. I am indebted for them to
my dear old friend, Mr. C. H. Stephenson, of
Lavender Hill, who has also kindly furnished me
with the notes on page 81. The *Barber's News* is
founded on an incident in the life of Stephen
Kemble, who, having fallen overboard from a boat,
was taken for a whale, crocodile, or other terrible
monster of the deep,—EDMUND GOLDSMID.

SATYR UPON WOMEN.

By Mr. James Robson.

THIS song is imperfectly compiled from part of a
" Satyr upon Women," wrote in Preston prison,
ſn 1715, by Mr. James Robson, a freeholder in
Thropton, near Rothbury, Northumberland, at
that time a musician in the rebel army. He
sung the Satyr aloud, at an iron barred window
looking into a garden, where a lady and her
maid were walking: after the song was finished,
the former says, " That young man seems very
severe upon our sex ; but perhaps he is singing
more from oppression than pleasure ; go give
him that half-crown piece," which the girl gave
him through the grating, at a period when he
was at the point of starving.

 ALL men of high and low degree,
  Come listen to my song ;
 The subject suits both you and me,
  With attestations strong :

Therefore I hope you'll not be nice,
    Attention true to pay,
And hence adhere to my advice,
    Lest you be led astray.

Should you to marry be inclin'd,
    I charge you to beware ;
And caution you to change your mind,
    Thus to escape that snare ;
Be not decoy'd by age nor youth,
    Whose aims are artfull all ;
But take my word as standard truth,
    You here may stand or fall.

If you should wed one with a dower,
    Obedience you must pay;
Or if you marry one who's poor,
    In rags you must array:
If you a blooming beauty wed,
    A cuckold you must be ;
And if a brunet blight your bed,
    You'll blush when belles you see.

Should you select a learned lass,
    Impertinence must pall ;
Or cull one from a vulgar class,
    She balderdash will bawl :

If you adopt a daft town's dame,
   Her behests will be bold :
Or coax one of inferior fame,
   She'll curse, carouse, and scold.

Shun lofty looks, and language loud,
   No stripes such tongues can tame ;
Fly wanton wenches mirthful mood,
   Which counsel can't reclaim :
A wife of stature tall will dare,
   To drag a giant down ;
And little women wicked are,
   One crop'd strong Samson's crown.

Reflect that Adam's innocence,
   Was to Eve's blunder blind ;
Whose crafty crime caus'd to commence,
   A curse upon mankind ;
So you cannot too cautious be,
   Of wormwood mix'd with gall ;
Then friends pray be advis'd by me,
   To wed with *none at all !*

BARBER'S NEWS,

OR

Shields in an Uproar.

A NEW SONG.

Tune—*"O the Golden Days of good Queen Bess."*

GREAT was the consternation,
　amazement and dismay, Sir,
Which, both in North and South Shields,
　prevail'd the other day, Sir ;
Quite panic-struck the natives were,
　when told by the barber,
That a terrible Sea Monster
　had got into the harbour,
" Have you heard the news, Sir?"
　" What news, pray master barber ?"
" Oh a terrible Sea Monster
　has got into the harbour !

Now each honest man in Shields—
 I mean both North and South, sir,
Delighting in occasions
 To expand their eyes and mouth, Sir :
And fond of seeing marv'lous sights,
 ne'er stay'd to get his beard off;
But ran to view the monster,
 its arrival, when he heard of.
Oh ! who could think of shaving
 when inform'd by the barber,
That a terrible Sea Monster
 had got into the harbour.

Each wife pursu'd her husband,
 and every child its mother,
Lads and lasses helter skelter,
 scamper'd after one another ;
Shopkeepers and mechanics too,
 forsook their daily labours,
And ran to gape and stare among
 their gaping staring neighbours.
All crowded to the river side,
 when told by the barber,
That a terrible Sea Monster
 had got into the harbour.

It happens very frequently
 That barber's news is fiction, Sir,
But the wond'rous news this morning
 was truth no contradiction, Sir ;

A something sure enough was there
  among the billows flouncing,
. Now sinking in the deep profound,
  now on the surface bouncing.
True as Gazette or Gospel
  were the tidings of the barber,
That a terrible Sea Monster
  had got into the harbour.

Some thought it was a shark, Sir,
  a porpus some conceived it ;
Some said it was a grampus,
  and some a whale believ'd it ;
Some swore, it was a sea horse,
  then own'd themselves mistaken,
For now they'd got a nearer view—
  'twas certainly a kraken.
Each sported his opinion,
  from the parson to the barber,
Of the terrible Sea Monster
  they had got in the harbour.

" Belay, belay," a sailor cried,
  "what that, this thing, a kraken !
'Tis no more like one, split my jib,
  than it is a flitch of bacon !
I've often seen a hundred such,
  all sporting in the Nile, Sir,
And you may trust a sailor's word,
  it is a crocodile, Sir."

Each strait to Jack knocks under,
　from the parson to the barber,
And all agreed a crocodile
　had got into the harbour.

Yet greatly Jack's discovery
　his auditors did shock, Sir,
For they dreaded that the salmon
　Would be eat up by the croc, Sir:
When presently the Crocodile,
　their consternation crowning,
Raised its head above the waves,
　And cried, " Help! O Lord, I'm drowning!"
Heavens! how their hair, sir, stood on end,
　from the parson to the barber ;
To find a speaking crocodile
　had got into the harbour.

This dreadful exclamation
　appall'd both young and old, Sir,
In the very stoutest hearts, indeed,
　It made the blood run cold, Sir ;
Ev'en Jack, the hero of the Nile,
　it caus'd to quake and tremble,
Until, an old wife, sighing, cried
　" Alas ! 'tis Stephen K———."
Heav'ns ! however all astonish'd,
　from the parson to the barber
To find that Stephen K———
　was the monster in the harbour.

Strait crocodilish fears gave place
   to manly gen'rous strife, Sir,
Most willingly each lent a hand
   to save poor Stephen's life, Sir ;
They drag'd him gasping to the shore,
   impatient for his history.
For how he came in that sad plight,
   to them was quite a mystery.
Tears glisten'd, Sir, in every eye,
   from the parson to the barber
When, swoln to thrice his natural size,
   they drag'd him from the harbour.

Now having roll'd and rubb'd him well
   an hour upon the beach, Sir,
He got upon his legs again,
   and made a serious speech, Sir ;
Quoth he, " An ancient proverb says,
   and true it will be found, Sirs,
Those born to prove an airy doom,
   will surely never be drown'd, Sirs.
For fate, Sirs, has us all in tow,
   from the monarch to the barber ;
Or surely I had breathed my last
   this morning in the harbour.

" Resolv'd to cross the river, Sirs,
   a sculler did I get into,
May Jonah's ill luck be mine,
   another when I step into !

Just when we'd reach'd the deepest part,
   O horror ! there it founders,
And down went poor Pillgarlick
   amongst the crabs and flounders !
But fate that keeps us all in tow,
   from the monarch to the barber,
Ordain'd I should not breathe my last
   this morning in the harbour.

" I've broke down many a stage coach,
   and many a chaise and gig, Sirs,
Once, in passing through a trap-hole,
   I found myself too big, Sirs,
I've been circumstane'd most oddly,
   while contesting hard a race, Sirs,
But ne'er was half so frighten'd,
   as amongst the crabs and plaice, Sirs.
O fate, Sirs, keeps us all in tow,
   from the monarch to the barber,
Or certainly I'd breathed my last,
   this morning in the harbour.

" My friends, for your exertions,
   my heart o'erflows with gratitude,
O may it prove the last time,
   you find me in that latitude ;
God knows with what mischances dire,
   the future may abound, Sirs,
But I hope and trust I'm one of those,
   not fated to be drown'd, Sirs,"

Thus ended his oration, Sir,
  I had it from the barber ;
And dripping, like some River God,
  he slowly left the harbour.

Ye men of North and South Shields too,
  God send ye all prosperity,
May your commerce ever flourish,
  Your stately ships still crowd the sea :
Unrivall'd in the coal trade,
  till doomsday may you stand sirs,
And every hour, fresh wonders,
  Your eyes and mouths expand, Sirs,
And long may Stephen K—— live,
  and never may the barber
Mistake him for a monster more,
  deep floundering in the harbour.

THE

Yorkshire Garland;

BEING A

CURIOUS COLLECTION

OF

OLD AND NEW SONGS,

Concerning that famous County.

YORK :

Printed for N. FROBISHER; and sold by J. LANGDALE,
NORTHALLERTON.
MDCCLXXXVIII.

Licensed and entered according to order.

"Give me the writing of the Songs,
and you may make the laws."

FLETCHER OF SALTOUN.

CONTENTS.

I. Yorke, Yorke, for my Monie   .   101

II. The Horse Race   110

III. The Bowes Tragedy   113

IV. A True and Tragical Song concerning
      Captain John Bolton, etc   .   .   125

V. In Praise of Yarm   .   .   128

VI. The Gamblers Fitted   .   .   .   130

THE
YORKSHIRE GARLAND,

SONG I.
A New Yorkshyre Song,

INTITULED:

Yorke, Yorke, for my monie :
Of all the Cities that ever I see,
For mery pastime and companie,
Except the Cittie of London.

As I came throw the Northe Countrey,
The fashions of the world to see
I sought for mery companie,
    To goe to the cittie of London :
And when to the cittie of Yorke I came,
I found good companie in the same,
Aswell disposed to every game,
    As if it had been at London.

Yorke, Yorke, for my monie,
 Of all the citties that ever I see,
For mery pastime and companie,
 Except the cittie of London.

And in that cittie what sawe I then?
 Knights, Squires, and Gentlemen,
A shooting went for matches ten,
 As if it had been at London.
And they shot for twentie poundes a bowe,
Besides great cheere they did bestowe,
I never sawe a gallanter showe,
 Except I had been at London,
  Yorke, Yorke, for my monie, &c.

These matches you shall understande
The earle of Essex tooke in hand,
Against the good earl of Cumberlande,
 As if it had been at London.
And agreede these matches all shall be,
For pastime and good companie,
At the cittie of Yorke full merily,
 As if it had been at London.
  Yorke, Yorke, for my monie, &c.

In Yorke there dwells an Alderman, which
Delites in shooting very much,
I never heard of any such,
 In all the cittie of London.

His name is Maltbie, mery and wise,
At any pastime you can devise,
But in shooting all his pleasure lyes,
    The like was never in London.
        Yorke, Yorke, for my monie, &c.

This Maltbie for the citties sake,
To shoote (himself) did undertake,
At any good match the earles would make,
    As well as they doe at London.
And he brought to the fielde with him,
One Specke, an archer proper and trim,
And Smith, that shoote about the pin,
    As if it had been at London.
        Yorke, Yorke, for my monie, &c.

Then came from Cumberland archers three,
Best bowmen in the north countree,
I will tell you their names what they be,
    Well knowne to the cittie of London.
Walmsley many a man doth knowe,
And Bolton how he draweth his bowe,
And Ratcliffes shooting long agoe,
    Well knowne to the cittie of London.
        Yorke, Yorke, &c.

And the noble earle of Essex came,
To the fielde himself to see the same,
Which shalbe had for ever in fame,
    As soone as I come at London.

For he shewed himself so diligent there,
To make a marke and keepe it faire :
It is worthie memorie to declare,
    Through all the cittie of London.
      Yorke, Yorke, &c.

And then was shooting out of crye,
The skantling at a handfull nie,
And yet the winde was very hie,
    As it is sometimes at London.
They clapt the cloutes so on the ragges,
There was such betting and such bragges :
And galloping up and down with nagges,
    As if it had been at London.
      Yorke, Yorke, &c.

And never an archer gave regarde,
To half a bowe, and half a yarde,
I never see matches goe more harde,
    About the cittie of London.
For fairer play was neuer plaide,
Nor fairer layes was neuer laide,
And a weeke together they kept this trade,
    As if it had been at London.
      Yorke, Yorke, &c.

The maior of Yorke, with his companie,
Were all in the fieldes, I warrant ye,
To see good rule kept orderly,
    As if it had been at London.

Which was a dutiful sight to see,
The Maior and Aldermen there to bee,
For the setting forth of Archerie,
    As well as they doe at London.
      Yorke, Yorke, &c.

And there was neither fault nor fray,
Nor any disorder any way;
But every man did pitch and pay,
    As if it had been at London.
As soone as every match was done;
Every man was paid that won,
And merily vp and downe did ronne,
    As if it had been at London.
      Yorke, Yorke, &c.

And neuer a man that went abroade,
But thought his monie well bestow'de;
And monie laid in heap and loade,
    As if it had been at London.
And Gentlemen there so franke and free,
As a mint at Yorke again should bee,
Like shooting did I never see,
    Except I had been at London.
      Yorke, Yorke, &c.

At Yorke were ambassadours three,
Of Russia, Lordes of high degree,
This shooting they desirde to see, .
    As if it had been at London.

And one desirde to draw a bowe,
The force and strength thereof to knowe,
And for his delight he drewe it so,
    As seldom seen in London.
      Yorke, Yorke, &c.

And they did maruaile very much,
There could be any archer such,
To shoote so farre the cloute to tutch,
    Which is no newes to London.
And they might well consider than,
An English shaft will kill a man,
As hath been proued where and whan,
    And chronicled since in London.
      Yorke, &c.

The earle of Cumberlands archers won,
Two matches cleare, ere all was done,
And I made hast a pace to ronne ;
    To carie these newes to London.
And Walmsley did the vpshot win,
With both his shafts so neere the pin,
You could scant have put three fingers in,
    As if it had been at London.
      Yorke, &c.

I passe not for my monie it cost,
Though some I spent and some I lost,
I wanted neither sod nor roast,
    As if it had been at London.

For there was plenty of euery thing,
Redd and fallowe deere, for a king,
I never sawe so mery shooting,
    Since first I came from London.
      Yorke, Yorke, &c.

God saue the cittie of Yorke therefore
That hath such noble friends in store
And such good aldermen send them more,
    And the like good luck at London.
For it is not little joye to see,
When Lordes and Aldermen so agree,
With such according communaltie,
    God sende vs the like at London.
      Yorke, Yorke, &c.

God saue the good earle of Cumberlande,
His praise in golden lines shall stande,
That maintaines archerie through the land,
    Aswell as they doe at London.
Whose noble minde so courteously,
Acquaintes himself with the communaltie
To the glory of his nobilitie,
    I will carie the praise to London.
      Yorke, Yorke, &c.

And tell the good earle of Essex thus,
As he is now yong and prosperous,
To vse such properties vertuous,
    Deserues great praise in London :

For it is no little joye to see,
When noble youthes so gracious bee,
To giue their good willes to their countrie,
    As well as they doe at London.
      Yorke, Yorke, &c.

Farewell good cittie of Yorke to thee,
Tell alderman Maltbie this from mee,
In print shall this good shooting bee,
    As soone as I come at London.
And many a Song will I bestowe,
On all the Musitians that I knowe ;
To sing the praises where they goe,
    Of the cittie of Yorke, in London.
      Yorke, Yorke, &c.

God save our Queene, and keep our peace,
That our good shooting maie increase :
And praying to God let vs not cease,
    As well at Yorke as at London.
That all our countrey round about,
May have archers good to hit the clout,
Which England cannot be without,
    No more than Yorke or London,
      Yorke, Yorke, &c.

God graunt that (once) her majestie,
Would come her cittie of Yorke to see,
For the comfort great of that countree,
    As well as she doth at London.

Nothing shalbe thought to deare,
To see her highnes person there,
With such obedient loue and feare,
   As ever she had in London.
Yorke, Yorke, for my momie,
   Of all the citties that ever I see,
For mery pastime and companie,
   Except the cittie of London.

From Yorke, by W. E. [William Elderton.]
(Originally) Imprinted at London by Richard
Jones; dwelling neere Holburne Bridge, 1584.

SONG II.

The Horse Race,

You heard how Gatherly race was run,
What horses lost, what horses won,
And all things else that there was done,
               That day.

Now of a new race I shall you tell,
Was neither run for bowl nor bell,
But for a great wager, as it befell,
               Men say.

Three gentlemen of good report
This race did make, to make some sport;
To which great company did resort,
               With speed.

To start them then they did require,
A gallant youth a brave esquire,
Who yielded soon to their desire,
               Indeed.

They started were, as I heard tell,
With, now St. George! God speed you well!
Let every man look to himsell,
               For me.

From Sever-Hill to Popleton Ash,
These horses run with spur and lash,
Through mire and sand and dirt dish dash,
              All three.

Bay Corbet first the start he got,
A horse well known all firy hot;
But he full soon his fire had shot;
              What tho'?

For he was out of graith so sore,
He could not run as heretofore,
Nor ne'er will run so any more,
              I trow.

Gray Ellerton then got the lead,
A gallant beast, of mickle speed;
For he did win the race indeed;
              Even so.

Grey Appleton the hindmost came,
And yet the horse was not to blame,
The rider needs must have the shame,
              For that.

For tho' he chanc'd to come behind,
Yet did he run his rider blind;
He was a horseman o' th' right kind,
              That's flat.

For when the race was past and done ;
He knew not who had lost nor won,
For he saw neither moon nor sun,
                    As then.

And thus this race is at an end
And so farewell to foe and friend :
God send us joy unto our end.
                    Amen.

The Patern of True Love;

OR

Bowes Tragedy.

Being a true Relation of the Life and Death of
Roger Wrightson and Martha Railton, of the
town of Bowes, in the County of York:
Shewing how the young man fell sick on
Shrove-Tuesday the 27th of February last
[1715], and dyed the 13th of March following:
Wherein is set forth the hard usage which the
young woman met with during the time of his
sickness; and upon hearing the first toll of the
passing bell, she fainted away; but by the
shriekes and cries of her mother and a young
woman, call'd her back again, and in amazed
condition continued about 12 hours, and then
she dyed. Also the weeping lamentation made
by both [their] friends at the grave, wherein
she was first decently laid, and then him;

being a fit pattern for all young men and women to prove constant in love; with a word of advice to all hard-hearted parents, not to cross their children in love. N.B. He was observed to say three times (just before he dyed) Martha, Martha, come away.

Love is stronger than Life.

A Patern of True Love, &c.

ROGER WRIGHTSON, at the sign of the Kings head in Bowes, near Bernard Castle, in Yorkshire,* courted Widow Railton's daughter, at the sign of the George in the same town, and has done more than a year. On Shrove-Tuesday, 1715, he fell sick, and languished till Sunday next but one following, and then dyed.

Poor Martha (for that was the maids name, whom he courted) Railton, tho' privately, took heavily on all that time, and only had declared to her sister and mother, that if he dyed, she could not live. An honest friend is unworthily blam'd for doing what I would have done myself, had I known it; for Martha Railton begged of him to go and see young Roger, and tell him she would gladly come and see him, if he thought fit, (knowing all his Father's family was against her). Roger answered, Nay, nay, T—my, our folks will be mad, but tell her I hope I shall recover. Well, the poor lass almost dead in sorrow, first sent an

---

* That is, Bowes in Yorkshire. Barnard Castle is in Durham.

orange, but Roger's mother sent it back; yet about three days before his death, Martha went: His mother was so civil as to leave her by his bedside, and ordered her danghter Hannah to come away, but she would not:—Poor Martha wanted only to speak three words to him, and (altho' she stayed two hours) yet Hannah would not let her have an opportunity, and so in a sorrowful manner she left him. Her book was her constant work, Friday, Saturday, Sunday; and she would oft say to herself, Oh! yon Hannah! if he dyes my heart will burst. So on the same Sunday se'night, at five o'clock in the afternoon, the bell was toll'd for him, and upon the first toll, Martha lay by her book, got her Mother in her arms, with Oh! dear mother, he's dead, I cannot live. About three minutes after, Thomas Petty * went in, and desired her to bee more easie: Her answer was, nay, now my heart is burst; and so in mournful cries and prayers was fainter and fainter for about three hours, and seemed to breath her last, but her mother and another girl of the town, shrick'd aloud, and so called her back again, (as they term it) and in amazed manner, distorted with convulsion fits, (just as it is described in Dr·

---

* The friend, as it should seem, who carried the message as before related.

Taylor's Holy Living and Dying) stayed her spirit 10 or 12 hours longer, and then she dyed.

At last things was brought to this issue, to be buried both in one grave, and the corps met at the Church gate, but Hannah objected against their being buried together, as also she did at her being laid first in the grave; but was answered that a bride was to go first to bed; she being asked why she should be so proud and inhumane: answered, that the said Martha might have taken fairer on, or have been hang'd. But Oh! the loud mourning of friends on both sides, at the corps meeting, and more at the grave; wherein first she was decently laid, and then he.

Bowes Tragedy, etc.

Being a true Relation of the Lives and Characters
of Roger Wrightson and Martha Railton, of the
Town of Bowes, in the County of ' York,' who
died for the Love of each other, in March last.

Tune of *Queen Dido*.

Good Christian people pray attend,
   To what I do in sorrow sing,
My bleeding heart is like to rend,
   At the sad tydings which I bring:
Of a young couple, whom cruel fate
Design'd to be unfortunate.

Let Carthage Queen be now no more
   The subject of your mournful song;
Nor such odd tales which heretofore,
   Did so amuse the teeming throng;
Since the sad story which I'll tell,
All other tragedys excell.

Yorkshire, the ancient town of Bowes,
   Of late did Roger Wrightson dwell;
He courted Martha Railton, who
   In vertuous works did most excell:
Yet Rogers friends would not agree,
That he to her should married be.

Their love continued one whole year,
   Full sore against their parents will;
And when he found them so severe,
   His royal heart began to chill:
And last Shrove-Tuesday, took his bed,
With grief and woe incompassed.

Thus he continued twelve days space,
   In anguish and in grief of mind:
And no sweet rest in any case,
   This ardent lovers heart could find:
But languished in a train of grief,
Which pierc'd his heart beyond relief.

Martha with anxious thoughts possest,
   A private messuage to him sent,
Acquainting him she could not rest,
   Untill she had seen her loving friend:
His answer was, "Nay, nay, my dear,
"Our folks will angry be I fear."

Full frought with grief she took no rest,
  But spent her time in pain and fear,
Untill few days before her death ;
  She sent an orange to her dear ;
But 's cruel mother, in disdain,
Did send the orange back again.

Three days before her lover dy'd,
  Poor Martha with a bleeding heart ;
To see her dying lover hy'd,
  In hopes to ease him of his smart :
Where she 's conducted to the bed,
In which this faithful young man laid.

Where she with doleful cries beheld,
  Her fainting lover in dispair ;
Which did her heart with sorrow fill,
  Small was the comfort she had there ;
Tho's mother show'd her great respect,
His sister did her much reject.

She staid two hours with her dear,
  In hopes for to declare her mind ;
But Hannah Wrightson stood so near,
  No time to do it she could find :
So that be'ng almost dead with grief,
Away she went without relief.

Tears from her eyes did flow amain,
  And she full oft wou'd sighing say,
" My constant love, alas ! is slain,
  " And to pale death become a prey :
" Oh! Hannah, Hannah, thou art base ;
" Thy pride will turn to foul disgrace."

She spent her time in godly prayers,
  And quiet rest from her did fly;
She to her friends full oft declares,
  She could not live if he did dye :
Thus she continued till the bell,
Began to sound his fatal knell.

And when she heard the dismal sound,
  Her godly book she cast away,
With bitter cries wou'd pierce the ground,
  Her fainting heart began 't decay.
She to her pensive mother said,
" I cannot live now he is dead."

Then after three short minutes space,
  As she in sorrow groaning lay;
A gentleman* did her imbrace,
  And mildly unto her did say,
" Dear melting soul be not so sad,
" But let your passion be allay'd."

---

* This gentleman was Thomas Petty. See preface.

Her answer was, " My heart is burst,
" My span of life is near an end ;
" My love from me by death is forc'd,
" My grief no soul can comprehend."
Then her poor heart did soon wax faint,
When she had ended her complaint.

For three hours space as in a trance,
   This broken-hearted creature lay,
Her mother wailing her mischance,
   To pacify her did essay :
But all in vain, for strength being past,
She seemingly did breath her last.

Her mother thinking she was dead,
   Began to strike and cry amain ;
And heavy lamentation made,
   Which call'd her spirits back again :
To be an object of hard fate,
And give to grief a longer date.

Distorted with convulsions, she
   In dreadful manner gasping lay,
Of twelve long hours no moment free,
   Her bitter groans did all dismay :
Then her poor heart b'ing sadly broke,
Submitted to the fatal stroke.

When things was to this issue brought,
  Both in one grave was to be laid :
But flinty hearted Hannah thought,
  By stubborn means for to persuade
Their friends and neighbours from the same,
For which she surely was to blame.

And being ask'd the reason why,
  Such base objections she did make ;
She answered thus scornfully,
  In words not fit for Billingsgate :
" She might have taken fairer on,
" Or else be hang'd :" Oh! heart of stone.

What hellborn fury had possest
  Thy vile inhumane spirit thus ?
What swelling rage was in thy breast,
  That could occasion this disgust ?
And make thee show such spleen and rage,
Which life can't cure, nor death asswage.

Sure some of Satan's minor imps,
  Ordained was to be thy guide :
To act the part of sordid pimps,
  And fill thy heart with haughty pride ;
But take this caveat once for all,
Such dev'lish pride must have a fall.

But when to church the corps was brought,
  And both of them met at the gate ;
What mournful tears by friends was shed,
  When that alas ! it was too late?
When they in silent grave was laid,
Instead of pleasing marriage bed.

You parents all both far and near,
  By this sad story warning take ;
Nor to your children be severe,
  When they their choice in love do make ;
Let not the love of cursed gold,
True lovers from their love with hold.

SONG IV.

A True and Tragical Song,

CONCERNING

CAPTAIN JOHN BOLTON,

OF BULMER, NEAR CASTLE-HOWARD;

Who, after a Trial of nine hours, at YORK-CASTLE, on Monday, the 27th of March, 1775, for the wilful Murther of ELIZABETH RAIN-BOW, an Ackwoth girl, his apprentice, was found guilty, and immediately received sentence to be executed at Tyburn, near York, on Wednesday following; but on the same morning, he strangled himself in the cell where he was confined, and so put a period to his wicked and desperate life. His body was then, pursuant to his sentence, given to the surgeons at York Infirmary, to be dissected and anatomized.

Tune of " *Fair Lady, lay your costly robes aside.*"

Good Christian people all, both old and young,
Pray give attention to this tragic song:
My days are short'ned by my vicious life,
And I must leave my children and my wife.

When I was prisoner to York-Castle brought,
My mind was fill'd with dismal, pensive thought ;
Conscious of guilt, it fill'd my heart with woe ;
Such terrors I before did never know.

When at the bar of justice I did stand,
With guilty conscience and uplifted hand,
The Court straightway then unto me they said,
What say you Bolton to the charge here laid?

In my defence I for a while did plead,
Sad sentence to evade (which I did dread)
But my efforts did me no kind of good,
For I must suffer and pay blood for blood.

To take her life I did premeditate ;
Which now has brought me to this wretched fate.
And may my death on all a terror strike,
That none may ever after do the like.

Murder prepense it is the worst of crimes,
And calls aloud for vengeanee at all times,
May none hereafter be like me undone,
But always strive the tempter's snares to shun.

By me she was seduc'd in her life time,
Which added guilt to guilt and crime to crime.
By me she was debauched and defil'd,
And then by me was murder'd, and her child.

Inhuman and unparallel'd the case,
I pray God give all mortal men more grace,
None's been more vile, more guilty in the land,
How shall I at the great tribunal stand?

I should have been her guardian and her friend,
I did an orphan take her for that end,
But satan did my morals so subdue,
That I did take her life and infant's too.

To poison her it was my full intent,
But Providence did that design prevent,
Then by a rope, fast twisted with a fife,
I strangled her and took her precious life.

My councel I did hope would get me clear,
But such a train of proofs there did appear,
Which made the court and jury for to cry,
He's guilty, let the wicked culprit die.

When I in fetters in York-Castle lay,
The morning of my execution day,
For to prevent the multitude to see
Myself exposed on the fatal tree,

I then did perpetrate my last vile crime,
And put a final end unto my time,
Myself I strangled in the lonesome cell,
And ceased in this transit world to dwell.

SONG V.

In Praise of Yarm.

Leave courts and great cities, vexation and care,
At Yarm all is peaceful, health breathes in the air,
The street clean and spacious, the houses are neat,
And the goddess Minerva has fix'd here her seat :
    Content, independent, serene and at ease,
    Come trace the green verdure of sweet wind-
      ing Tees.

Here plentiful prospects are seen all around,
Rich merchants dispersing the fruits of the ground;
Here honour and commerce sincerely unite,
The ladies are charming, the merchants polite :
    Content, independent, serene, and at ease,
    Come trace the green verdure by sweet wind-
      ing Tees.

See snowy flocks feeding on every hill,
Soft zephirs blow gentle, and cooing doves bill ;
Each sense is delighted, all nature looks gay ;
And this month of October * seems blooming as
  May :

---

* 1765.

Content, independent, serene and at ease,
Come trace the green verdure by sweet winding Tees.

Now winter approaches, should stormy winds
blow,
The mountains and valleys be covered with snow,
The muse shall sing oft, the dull vapours to
charm,
Ill spleen and black envy shall fly far from Yarm:
Content, independent, serene and at ease,
Come trace the green verdure by sweet wind-
ing Tees.

Vauxhall, masquerades, and assemblies I've seen,
And all the brighs circle surrounding a Queen,
But what is the splendour of court, or of town,
I can view nobler sights by the light of the moon:
Content, independent, serene and at ease,
Come trace the green verdure by sweet wind-
ing Tees.

What are stars, and gay garters, or titles and state,
Or the servile vain levees that pester the great?
Let me act but discreetly my little low part,
While virtue secures me a chearful good heart:
Content, independent, serene and at ease,
Let me trace the green verdure by sweet
winding Tees.

THE GAMBLERS FITTED.

You sportsmen all, both old and young,
Come listen now unto my song,
It is of a foot race which was run,
At Drax in Yorkshire by two men.
                  To my fa, da, la, &c.

One of whose names it was C—s W—r,
Not a great runner, but a great talker,
'Tother Eclipse a man of fame,
For by his running he got that name.

On the twenty-fifth day of August,
The time appointed that run they must,
Where a great many people did resort,
To Drax to see the famous sport.

When many people was come there,
They some of them begun to fear,
Says they no race we shall have I think,
For C——s has come without his jink.

But soon the money he did produce,
Or we shou'd have said it was his excuse,
O then says they now let's to place,
For I believe we shall have a race.

While the company staid in town,
They cry'd out Eclipse for half a crown,
No sooner into the field they came,
But the Gamblers all chang'd their name.

They cry'd out C—s for a pound or two,
Which made Drax people all look blue,
Oh says they our chance is ill,
For these must needs be men of skill.

They started but had not run half way,
Before C—s begun to shew foul play,
O then says Eclipse if that's the case,
I'll let thee see another pace.

Then Eclipse made a spring and left him soon,
Which made the gamblers to look down,   · ·
Upon that Drax people gave a shout,
And made poor C—s give running out.

O brave Eclipse thou hast won this race,
And brought this champion to disgrace,
Thy name shall be Eclipse for ever,
While Ch—s is nought but a deceiver.

So to conclude and end my song,
I hope the gamblers will think on,
And never shout with such a sound,
To lay a guinea to a pound.

If any of you I do offend,
With these few lines I now have penn'd,
I ask your pardon for the same,
But I'll conclude with Eclipse's fame,
    To my fa, da, la, da, la, da, la,
    lade, dou, dade, dou, de.

THE

Northumberland Garland;

OR,

NEWCASTLE NIGHTINGALE:

A

MATCHLESS COLLECTION

OF

FAMOUS SONGS.

OLD TYNE SHALL LISTEN TO MY TALE,
AND ECHO, DOWN THE BORDERING VALE,
THE LIQUID MELODY PROLONG. *Akenside.*

NEWCASTLE:

PRINTED BY AND FOR HALL AND ELLIOT.

MDCCXCIII.

Licensed and entered according to order.

"Read, mark, learn and inwardly
digest."

CONTENTS.

I. The Battle of Otterburn . 139

II. The Hunting of the Cheviat . . 153

III. The Hunting in Chevy-Chase . 165

IV. Fair ' Mabel ' of Wallington . . 176

V. A lamentable Ditty, made upon the
death of a worthy gentleman
named George Stoole . 181

VI. The Sickness, Death, and Burial, of
Eckys Mare. . . . 186

THE
Northumberland Garland.

SONG I.
The Battle of Otterburn.*

(NEAR 400 YEARS OLD.)

YT fell abowght the Lamasse tyde,
  Whan husbondes wynne ther haye,
The dowghtye Dowglasse bowynd him to ryde,
  In Ynglond to take a praye:

The yerlle of Fyffe, withowghten stryffe,
  He bowynd him over Sulway:
The grete wolde ever together ryde,
  That raysse they may rewe for aye.

Over 'Ottercap' hyll they cam in,
  And so dwyn by Rodelyffe crage,
Upon Grene 'Leyton' they lyghted dowyn,
  'Styrande many a' stage:

---

* Fought the 9th of August 1388.

And boldely brent Northumberlond,
  And haryed many a towyn;
They dyd owr Ynglyssh men grete wrange,
  To battell that were not bowyn.

Than spake a berne upon the bent,
  Of comforte that was not colde,
And sayd, We have brent Northomberlond,
  We have all welth in holde.

Now we have haryed all Bamboroweschyre,
  All the welth in the world have wee,
I rede we ryde to Newe Castell,
  So styll and stalwurthlye.

Upon the morowe, when it was day,
  The standerdes schone fulle bryght;
To the Newe Castell the toke the waye,
  And thether they cam full ryght.

Sir Henry Perssy laye at the New Castell,
  I tell yow withowtten drede;
He had byn a march-man all hys dayes,
  And kept Barwyke upon Twede.

To the New Castell when they cam,
  The Skotts they cryde on hyght,
Syr Hary Perssy, and thou byste within,
  Com to the fylde, and fyght:

For we have brente Northomberlonde,
  Thy erytage good and ryght ;
And syne my logeyng I have take,
  With my brande dubbyd many a knyght.

Sir Harry Perssy came to the walles,
  The Skottysh oste for to se ;
And sayd, And thou hast brent Northomberlond,
  Full sore it rewyth me.

Yf thow hast haryed all Bamboroweschyre,
  Thow hast done me grete envye ;
For the trespasse thow hast me done,
  The tone of us schall dye.

Where schall I byde the, sayd the Dowglas,
  Or where wylte thow com to me?
" At Otterborne in the hygh way,
  Ther mast thow well logeed be.

The roo full rekeless ther she runnes,
  To make the game and glee :
The fawken and the fesaunt both,
  Among the holtes on hye.

Ther mast thow have thy welth at wyll,
  Well looged ther mast be ;
Yt schall not be long, or I com the tyll,"
  Sayd syr Harry Perssye.
    T

Ther schall I byde the, sayd the Dowglas,
  By the fayth of my bodye.
Thether schall I com, sayd syr Harry Perssy
  My trowth I plyght to the.

A pype of wyne he gave them over the walles,
  For soth, as I yow saye :
Ther he mayd the Dowglasse drynke,
  And all hys ost that daye.

The Dowglas turnyd hym homewarde agayne,
  For soth withowghten naye,
He took his logeynge at Oterborne
  Upon a Wedynsday :

And ther he pyght his standerd dowyn,
  Hys gettyng more and lesse,
And syne he warned his men to goo
  To chose ther geldynges gresse.

A Skottysshe knyght hoved upon the bent
  A wache I dare well saye :
So was he ware on the noble Perssy,
  In the dawnyng of the daye.

He prycked to his pavyleon dore,
  As fast as he might ronne,
Awaken, Dowglas, cryed the knyght
  For hys love that syttes in trone

Awaken, Dowglas, cryed the knyght,
　For thow maste waken wyth wynne;
Yender have I spyed the prowde Perssye,
　And seven standardes with hym.

Nay, by my trowth, the Dowglas sayed,
　It ys but a fayned taylle :
He durst not loke on my brede banner,
　For all Ynglonde so haylle.

Was I not yesterdaye at the Newe Castell,
　That stondes so fayre on Tyne?
For all the men the Perssy had,
　He cowde not garre me ones to dyne.

He stepped owt at his pavelyon dore,
　To loke and it were lesse;
" Araye yow, lordynges, one and all,
　For here bygynnes no peysse.

The yerle of Mentaye, thow art my eme,
　The fowarde I gyve to the :
The yerlle of Huntlay cawte and kene,
　He schall ' wyth the be.'

The lord of Bowghan in armure bryght,
　On the other hand he schall be :
Lorde Jhonstone and lorde Maxwell,
　They to schall be with me.

Swynton fayre fylde upon your pryde
  To batell make yow bowen :
Syr Davy Skotte, syr Water Stewarde,
  Syr Jhon of Agurstone.

A Fytte.

THE Perssy came before hys oste,
  Whych was ever a gentyll knyght.
Upon the Dowglas lowde can he crye,
  I wyll holde that I have hyght :

For thow haste brente Northomberlonde,
  And done me grete envye ;
For thys trespasse thou hast me done,
  The tone of us schall dye.

The Dowglas answerde hym agayne,
  With grete wurdes upon hye,
And sayd, I have twenty agaynst 'thy' one
  Byholde and thou maste see.

With that the Perssye was greyved sore
  For soth as I yow saye :
He lyghted dowyn upon hys foote,
  And schoote hys horsse clene away.

Every man sawe that he did soo,
  That rall was ever in rowght ;
Every man schoote hys horsse hym froo,
  And lyght hym rowynde abowght.

Thus syr Hary Perssye toke the fylde,
    For soth, as I yow saye :
Jesu Cryste in heven on hyght
    Dyd helpe hym well that daye.

But nyne thowzand, ther was no moo ;
    The cronykle wyll not layne :
Forty thowsande Skottes and fowre
    That daye fowght them agayne.

But when the battell byganne to joyne,
    In hast ther cam a knyght,
The letters fayr furth hath he tayne,
    And thus he sayd full ryght :

My lorde, your father he gretes yow well,
    With many a noble knyght ;
He desyres yow to byde
    That he may see thys fyght.

The baron of Grastoke ys com owt of the west,
    Wyth hym a noble companye ;
All they loge at your fathers thys nyght,
    And the battel fayne wolde they see.

For Jesus love, sayd syr Harye Perssy,
    That dyed for yow and me,
Wende to my lorde my father agayne,
    And saye thow sawe me not with yee.

My trowth ys plyght to yonne Skottyssh knyght,
   It nedes me not to layne :
That I schulde byde hym upon thys bent,
   And I have hys trowth agayne :

And if that I wynde off thys growende,
   For soth onfowghten awaye,
He wolde me call but a kowarde knyght
   In hys londe another daye.

Yet had I lever to be rynde and rente,
   By Mary that mykell maye,
Then ever my manhood schulde be reprovyd
   Wyth a Skotte another day.

Wherfore, schote, archars, for my sake,
   And let scharpe arowes flee :
Mynstrells, playe up for your waryson,
   And well quyt it schall be.

Every man thynke on hys trewe love,
   And marke hym to the Trenite :
For to God I make myne avowe
   This daye wyll I not fle.

The blodye harte in the Dowglas armes,
   Hys standerde stode on hye ;
That every man myght full well knowe,
   By syde stode starres thre.

The whyte lyon on the Ynglyssh perte,
　Forsoth as I yow sayne ;
The lusettes and the 'cresawntes' both ;
　The Skottes fowght them agayne.

Upon sent Andrewe lowde can they crye,
　And thrysse they schowte on ayght,
And syne marked them one owr Ynglysshe men,
　As I have tolde yow ryght.

Sent George the bryght, owr ladyes knyght,
　To name they were full fayne ;
Owr Ynglyssh men they cryde on hyght,
　And thrysse they schowtte agayne.

Wyth that scharpe arowes bygan to flee,
　I tell yow in sertayne ;
Men of armes byganne to joyne ;
　Many a dowghty man was ther slayne.

The Perssy and the Dowglas mette,
　That ather of other was fayne ;
They 'swapped' together whyll that the swette,
　With swordes of fine collayne ;

Tyll the bloode from ther bassonettes ranne,
　As the roke doth in the rayne.
Yelde the to me, sayd the Dowglas,
　Or elles thow schalt be slayne ;

For I see, by thy bryght bassonet,
  Thow arte sum man of myght ;
And so I do by thy burnysshed brande,
  Thow art an yerle, or elles a knyght.

By my good faythe, sayd the noble Perssye,
  Now haste thou rede full ryght,
Yet wyll I never yelde me to the,
  Whyll I may stonde and fyght.

They swapped together, whyll that they swette,
  Wyth swordes scharpe and long ;
Ych on other so faste thee beette,
  Tyll ther helmes cam in peyses dowyn.

The Perssy was a man of strenghth,
  I tell yow in thys stounde,
He smote the Dowglas at the swordes length,
  That he felle to the growynde.

The sworde was scharpe and sore can byte,
  I telle yow in sertayne ;
To the harte he cowde him smyte,
  Thus was the Dowglas slayne.

The stonderdes stode styll on ' elke' asyde,
  With many grevous grone ;
Ther they fowght the day, and all the nyght,
  And many a dowghty man was slayne,
U

Ther was no freke that ther wolde flye,
  But styffely in stowre can stond,
Ych one hewyng on other whyll they myght drye
  Wyth many a baylleful bronde.

Ther was slayne upon the Skottes syde,
  For soth and sertenly,
Syr James a Dowglas ther was slayne,
  That daye that he cowde dye.

The yerlle of Mentaye he was slayne,
  Grysely groned uppon the growynd;
Syr Davy Skotte, syr Walter Stewarde,
  Syr 'john' of Agurstonne.

Syr Charlles Morrey in that place
  That never a fote wold flee;
Sir Hugh Maxwell, a lorde he was,
  With the Dowglas dyd he dye.

Ther was slayne upon the Skottes syde,
  For soth as I yow saye,
Of fowre and forty thowsande Skottes,
  Went but eyghtene awaye.

Ther was slayne upon the Ynglisshe syde,
  For soth and sertenlye,
A gentell knyght, sir John 'Fitzhewe,'
  Yt was the more pety.

Syr James Harebotell ther was slayne,
  For hym ther hartes were sore,
The gentyll ' Lovell' ther was slayne
  That the Perssys standerd bore.

Ther was slayne upon the Ynglyssh perte,
  For soth as I yow saye ;
Of nyne thowsand Ynglyssh men,
  Fyve hondert cam awaye :

The other were slayne in the fylde,
  Cryste kepe ther sowlles from wo,
Seyng ther was so fewe fryndes
  Agaynst so many a foo.

Then on the morne they mayde them beerys
  Of byrch, and haysell graye ;
Many a wydowe with wepyng teyres
  Ther makes they fette awaye,

Thys fraye bygan at Otterborne
  Bytwene the nyghte and the day :
Ther the Dowglas lost hys lyffe,
  And the Perssye was lede awaye.

Then was ther a Scottyssh prisoner tayne,
  Syr Hewe Mongomery was hys name,
For soth as I yow saye,
  He borowed the Perssy home agayne.

Now let us all for Perssy praye
  To Jesu most of myght,
To bryng hys sowlle to the blysse of heven,
  For he was a gentyll knyght.

SONG II.

The Hunting of the Cheviat.

(ABOUT 400 YEARS OLD.)

THE Persé owt off Northumbarlande,
  And a vowe to God mayd he,
That he wold hunte in the mountayns
  Of Chyviat within dayes thre ;
In the magger of doughté Dogles,
  And all that ever with him be.

The fattiste hartes in all Cheviat
  He sayd he wold kyll, and cary them away.
Be my feth, sayd the dougheti Doglas agayn,
  I wyll let that hontyng yf that I may.

Then the Persé owt of Banborowe cam,
  With hym a myghtee meany ;
With fifteen hondrith 'archares' bold, off blood
      and bone,
  The wear chosen owt of shyars thre.

This begane on a Monday at morn,
  In Cheviat the hillys so he ;
The chyld may rue that ys unborn,
  It was the mor pitté.

The dryvars thorowe the woodes went
  For to reas the dear ;
Bomen byckarte uppone the bent
  With ther browd aras cleare.

Then the wyld thorowe the woodes went
  On every syde shear ;
Grea hondes thorowe the grevis glent
  For to kyll thear dear.

The begane in Chyviat the hyls above
  Yerly on a sonny day ;
Be that it drewe to the oware off none
  A hondrith fat hartes ded ther lay.

The blewe a mort uppone the bent,
  The semblyd on sydis shear ;
To the quyrry then the Persé went
  To se the bryttlynge off the deare.

He sayd, It was the Duglas promys
  This day to meet me hear ;
But I wyste he wold faylle verament :
  A great oth the Persé swore.

At the last a squyar of ' Northomberlonde,'
   Lokyde at his hand full ny,
He was war ath the doughetie Doglas commynge,
   With him a myghtte meany.

Both with spear, byll, and brandę :
   Yt was a myghti sight to se,
Hardyar men both off hart nar hande
   Wear not in Christiantè.

The wear twenty hondrith spear-men good,
   Withowte any feale ;
The wear borne along be the watter a Twyde,
   Yth boundes of Tividale.

Leave off the brytlyng of the dear, he sayde,
   And to your bowys lock ye tayk good heed ;
For never sithe ye wear on your mothars borne
   Had ye never so mickle ned.

The dougheti Dogglas on a stede,
   He rode all his men beforne ;
His armor glytteryde as dyd a gledc ;
   A bolder barne was never born.

Tell me ' what' men ye ar, he says,
   Or whos men that ye be :
Who gave youe leave to hunte in this
   Chyviat chays in the spyt of me ?

The first mane that ever him an answear mayd,
  It was the good lord Persé :
We wyll not tell the 'what' men we ar, he says,
  Nor whos men that we be ;
But we will hount hear in this chays
  In the spyt of thyne and of the.

The fattiste hartes in all Chyviat
  We have kyld, and cast to cary them away.
Be my troth, sayd the doughté ' Dogglas' agayn,
  Ther for the ton of us shall de this day.

Then sayd the doughté Doglas
  Unto the lord Persé :
To kyll all these giltles men,
  Alas ! it were a great pittè.

But, Persé, thowe art a lord of lande,
  I am a yerle callyd within my contrè ;
Let all our men uppone a parti stande ;
  And do the battell off the and of me.

Now Christes cors on his crowne, sayd the lord
    Persé,
  Who soever ther to says nay.
Be my troth, dougghtté Doglas, he says,
  Thow shalt never se that day ;

Nether in Ynglonde, Skottlonde, nar France,
  Nor for no man of a woman born,
But and fortune be my chance,
  I dar met him on man for on,

Then bespayke a squyar of Northombarlonde,
  Ric. Wytharyngton was his nam ;
It shall never be tolde in Sothe Ynglonde, he says,
  To kyng Herry the fourth for sham.

I wat youe byn great lordes twaw,
  I am a poor squyar of lande ;
I wyll never se my captayne fyght on a fylde,
  And stand myselffe, and loocke on,
But whyll I may my weppone welde
  I wyll not [fayl] bothe harte and hande.

That day, that day, that dredfull day,
  The first fit here I fynde :
And youe wyll here any mor athe hountyng athe
     Chyviat,
  Yet ys ther mor behynd.

[FIT THE SECOND.]

THE Yngglyshe men hade ther bowys yebent,
  Ther hartes were good yenoughe ;
The first off arros that the shote off,
  Seven skore spear-men the sloughe.

Yet byddys the yerle Doglas uppon the bent,
  A captayne good yenoughe,
And that was sene verament,
  For he wrought them hom both woo and
    wouche.

W

The Dogglas pertyd his ost in thre,
  Lyk a cheffe cheften off pryde,
With suar speares off myghtte tre,
  The cum in on every syde.

Thrughe our Yngglishe archery
  Gave many a wounde full wyde,
Many a doughete the garde to dy,
  Which ganyde them no pryde.

The Ynglyshe men let thear 'bowys' be,
  And pulde owt brandes that wer bright ;
It was a hevy sight to se
  Bryght swordes on basnites lyght.

Thorowe ryche male, and myne-ye-ple,
  Many sterne the stroke done streght :
Many a freyke, that was full fre,
  Ther undar foot dyd lyght.

At last the Duglas and the Persé met,
  Lyk to captayns of myght and of mayne ;
The swapte togethar tyll the both swat
  With swordes that wear of fyn myllàn.

These worthé freckys for to fyght
  Ther to the wear full fayne,
Tyll the bloode owte off thear basnetes sprente,
  As ever dyd heal or ran.

'Holde' the, Persé, sayd the Doglas,
   And i feth I shall the brynge
Wher thowe shalte have a yerls wagis
   Of Jamy our 'Scottish' kynge.

Thoue shalte have thy ransom fre,
   I hight the hear this thinge,
For the manfullyste man yet art thowe,
   That ever I conqueryd in filde fightyng,

Nay, sayd the lorde Persé,
   I tolde it the beforne,
That I wolde never yeldyde be
   To no man of a woman born.

With that ther cam an arrowe hastely
   Forthe off a myghtté wane,
Hit hathe strekene the yerle Duglas
   In at the brest bane.

Thoroue lyvar and longs bathe
   The sharpe arrowe ys gane,
That never after in all his lyffe days
   He spayke mo wordes but ane,
That was, Fyghte ye, my myrry men, whyllys ye
     may,
   For my liff days ben gan.

The Persé leanyde on his brande,
   And sawe the Duglas de;
He tooke the dede mane be the hande,
   And sayd, Wo ys me for the!

To have savyde thy liffe I wold have pertyde with
  My landes for years thre ;
For a better man of hart, nare of hande,
  Was not in all the north contrè.

Off all that se a Skottishe knyght,
  Was callyd sir Hewe the Monggonbyrry,
He sawe the Duglas to the deth was dyght ;
  He spendyd a spear a trusti tre :

He rod uppon a corsiare
  Throughe a hondrith archery ;
He never stynttyde, nar never blane,
  Tyll he cam to the good lord Persè.

He set uppon the lord Persé,
  A dynte that was full soare ;
With a suar spear of a myghtté tre
  Clean thorow the body he the Persé ' bore.'

Athe tothar syde, that a man myght se,
  A large cloth yard and mare ;
Towe bettar captayns wear nat in Cristiantè,
  Than that day slain wear ther.

An archar of Northomberlonde
  Say slean was the lord Persè,
He bar a bende bow in his hand,
  Was made off trusti tre :

An arow, that a cloth yarde was lang,
  Toth hard stele hayld he ;
A dynt that was both sad and soar,
    Ie sat on sir Hewe the Monggonbyrry.

The dynt yt was both sad and sar,
  That he of Monggonberry sete ;
The swane-fethars, that his arrowe bar,
  With his hart blood the wear wete.

Ther was never a freake wone foot wolde fle,
  But still in stour dyd stand,
Heawyng on yche othar, whyll the myght dre,
  With many a balfull brande.

This battell begane in Chyviat,
  An owar before the none,
And when the even-song bell was rang,
  The battell was nat half done.

The tooke on ethar hand,
  Be the lyght off the mone ;
Many had no strenght for to stande,
  In Chyviat the hillys ' abone.'

Of fifteen hondrith archars of Ynglonde
  Went away but fifti and thre ;
Of twenty hondrith spear-men of Skotlonde,
  But even five and fifti.

But all wear slayne Cheviat within :
   The had no 'strengthe' to stand on hy ;
The chylde may rue that ys unborne,
   It was the mor pittè.

Thear was slayne with the lord Persé,
   Sir John of Agerstone,
Sir Rogar the hinde Hartly,
   Sir Wyllyam, the bolde Hearone.

Sir Jorg the worthé Lovele,
   A knyght of great renowen,
Sir Raff the ryche Rugbè,
   With dyntes wear beaten dowene.

For Wettharryngton my harte was wo,
   That ever he slayne shulde be ;
For when both his leggis wear hewyne in to,
   Yet he knyled and fought on hys kny.

Ther was slayne with the dougheti Duglas
   Sir Hewe the Monggonbyrry,
Sir Davy Lwdale that worthé was,
   His sistars son was he.

Sir Charls a Murré, in that place,
   That never a foot wolde flee ;
Sir Hewe Maxwell, a lorde he was,
   With the Doglas dyd he dey.

So on the morrowe the mayde them byears
   Off birch, and hasell so 'gray ;'
Many wedous, with wepyng tears,
   Cam to fach ther makys away.

Tivydale may carpe off care,
   Northombarlond may mayke 'great' mon,
For towe such captayns, as slayne wear thear,
   On the march perti shall never be non.

Word ys commen to Eddenburrowe
   To Jamy the Skottishe kyng,
That dougheti Duglas, lyff tenant of the merches,
   He lay slean Chyviot with in.

His handdes dyd he weal and wryng,
   He says, Alas, and woe ys me !
Such another captayn Skotland within,
   He sayd, yefeth shuld never be.

Worde is commyn to lovly Londone
   Till the fourth Harry our kyng,
That lord Persé, 'leyff'-tenante of the merchis,
   He lay slayne Chyviat within.

God have merci on his soll, sayd kyng Harry,
   Good lord, yf thy will it be !
I have a hondrith captayns in Ynglonde, he sayd,
   As good as ever was he :
But, Persé, and I brook my lyffe,
   Thy deth well quyte shall be.

As our noble kyng made his avowe,
  Like a noble prince of renowen,
For the deth of the lord Persè,
  He dyde the battell of Hombyll-down :

Where syx and thritté Skottish knyghtes
  On a day wear beaten down :
Glendale glytteryde on ther armor bryght,
  Over castill, towar, and town.

This was the hontynge off the Cheviat ;
  That tear begane this spurn :
Old men, that knowen the grownde well yenoug e,
  Call it the battell of Otterburn.

At Otterburn began this spurne
  Uppon a ' Monnyn' day :
Ther was the dougghté Doglas slean,
  The Persé never went away.

Ther was never a tym on the march partes,
  Sen the Doglas and the Persé met,
But yt was mervele, and the rede blude ronne no ,
  As the reane doys in the stret.

Jhesue Crist our balys bete,
  And to the blys us brynge !
Thus was the hountynge of the Chivyat ;
  God send us all good endyng !

The Hunting in Chevy-Chase.

GOD prosper long our noble king,
  Our lives and safeties all;
A woeful hunting once there did
  In Chevy-Chase befall.

To drive the deer with hound and horn,
  Earl Percy took his way;
The child may rue that is unborn
  The hunting of that day.

The stout earl of Northumberland
  A vow to God did make,
His pleasure in the Scottish woods
  Three summers days to take;

The chiefest harts in Chevy-chase
  To kill and bear away:
These tidings to Earl Douglas came,
  In Scotland where he lay;

X

Who sent earl Percy present word,
  He would prevent his sport :
The English earl, not fearing this,
  Did to the woods resort,

With fifteen hundred bowmen bold
  All chosen men of might,
Who knew full well, in time of need,
  To aim their shafts aright.

The gallant greyhounds swifty ran,
  To chase the fallow-deer ;
On Monday they began to hunt,
  When day-light did appear.

And, long before high-noon, they had
  A hundred fat bucks slain ;
Then, having din'd, the drovers went
  To rouse them up again.

The bowmen muster'd on the hills,
  Well able to endure ;
Their backsides all, with special care,
  That day were guarded sure.

The hounds ran swiftly through the woods,
  The nimble deer to take,
And with their cries the hills and dales
  An echo shrill did make.

Lord Percy to the quarry went,
   To view the slaughter'd deer ;
Quoth he, Earl Douglas promised,
   This day to meet me here :

If that I thought he would not come,
   No longer would I stay.
With that a brave young gentleman
   Thus to the earl did say :

Lo ! yonder doth earl Douglas come,
   His men in armour bright ;
Full twenty hundred Scotish spears
   All marching in our sight ;

All men of pleasant Tividale,
   Fast by the river Tweed.
Then cease your sport, earl Percy said,
   And take your bows with speed.

And now with me, my countrymen,
   Your courage forth advance ;
For never was there champion yet,
   In Scotland or in France,

That ever did on horseback come,
   But if mayhap it were,
I durst adventure, man for man,
   With him to break a spear.

Earl Douglas, on a milk-white steed,
  Most like a baron bold,
Rode foremost of the company,
  Whose armour shone like gold.

Show me, said he, whose men you be,
  That hunt so boldly here ;
That, without my consent, do chase,
  And kill my fallow deer.

The man that first did answer make,
  Was noble Percy, he ;
Who said, We list not to declare,
  Nor show whose men we be :

Yet we will spend our dearest blood,
  Thy chiefest harts to slay.
Then Douglas swore a solemn oath,
  And thus in rage did say :

Ere thus I will outbraved be,
  One of us two shall dye ;
I know thee well, an earl thou art,
  Lord Percy, so am I.

But trust me, Percy, pity it were,
  And great offenee to kill
And of these our harmless men,
  For they have done no ill.

Let thou and I the battle try,
  And set our men aside.
Accurs'd be he, Lord Percy said,
  By whom this is deny'd.

Then stepp'd a gallant squire forth,
  Witherington was his name,
Who said, I would not have it told
  To Henry our king, for shame,

That e'er my captain fought on foot,
  And I stood looking on :
You be two earls, said Witherington,
  And I a squire alone :

I'll do the best that do I may,
  While I have strength to stand ;
While I have pow'r to wield my sword,
  I'll fight with heart and hand.

Our English archers bent their bows,
  Their hearts were good and true ;
At the first flight of arrows sent,
  Full three-score Scots they slew.

To drive the deer with hound and horn
  Earl Douglas had the bent ;
A captain mov'd with mickle pride,
  The spears to shivers sent.

They clos'd full fast on every side,
  No slackness there was found ;
And many a gallant gentleman
  Lay gasping on the ground.

O Christ ! it was a grief to see,
  And likewise for to hear
The cries of men lying in their gore,
  And scatter'd here and there.

At last these two stout earls did meet,
  Like captains of great might ;
Like lions mov'd, they laid on load,
  And made a cruel fight.

They fought until they both did sweat,
  With swords of temper'd steel ;
Until the blood, like drops of rain,
  They trickling down did feel.

Yield thee, lord Percy, Douglas said,
  In faith I will thee bring,
Where thou shalt high advanced be
  By James our Scotish king :

Thy ransom I will freely give,
  And thus report of thee,
Thou art the most courageous knight
  That ever I did see.

No, Douglas, quoth earl Percy then,
  Thy proffer I do scorn ;
I will not yield to any Scot
  That ever yet was born.

With that there came an arrow keen,
  Out of an English bow,
Which struck earl Douglas to the heart,
  A deep and deadly blow ;

Who never spoke more words than these,
  Fight on my merry men all ;
For why, my life is at an end,
  Lord Percy sees my fall.

Then leaving life, earl Percy took
  The dead man by the hand,
And said, Earl Douglas, for thy life,
  Would I had lost my land !

O Christ ! my very heart doth bleed,
  With sorrow for thy sake;
For sure a more renowned knight
  Mischance did never take.

A knight amongst the Scots there was
  Which saw earl Douglas die,
Who straight in wrath did vow revenge
  Upon the earl Percy :

Sir Hugh Montgomery was he call'd ;
  Who with a spear most bright,
Well mounted on a gallant steed,
  Ran fiercely through the fight ;

And pass'd the English archers all,
  Without all dread or fear ;
And through earl Percy's body then
  He thrust his hateful spear :

With such a vehement force and might
  He did his body gore,
The spear went through the other side
  A large cloth-yard, and more.

So thus did both these nobles die,
  Whose courage none could stain ;
An English archer then perceiv'd
  The noble earl was slain :

He had a bow bent in his hand,
  Made of a trusty tree ;
An arrow of a cloth-yard long
  Up to the head drew he :

Against sir Hugh Montgomery,
  So right the shaft he set,
The grey-goose-wing that was thereon
  In his heart-blood was wet.

This fight did last from break of day
  Till setting of the sun ;
For when they rung the evening-bell
  The battle scarce was done.

With the earl Percy there was slain
  Sir John of Ogerton,
Sir Robert Ratcliffe, and sir John,
  Sir James that bold baron :

And, with sir George, and good sir James,
  Both knights of good account,
Good sir Ralph Raby there was slain,
  Whose prowess did surmount.

For Witherington needs must I wail,
  As one in doleful dumps ;
For when his legs were smitten off,
  He fought upon his stumps.

And with earl Douglas there was slain
  Sir Hugh Montgomery,
Sir Charles Currèl, that from the field
  One foot would never fly ;

Sir Charles Murrèl of Ratcliffe too,
  His sister's son was he ;
Sir David Lamb, so well esteem'd,
  Yet saved could not be.

Y

And the lord Maxwell, in like wise,
  Did with earl Douglas die :
Of twenty hundred Scotish spears
  Scarce fifty-five did fly,

Of fifteen hundred Englishmen,
  Went home but fifty-three :
The rest were slain in Chevy-chace,
  Under the greenwood tree.

Next day did many widows come,
  Their husbands to bewail :
They wash'd their wounds in brinish tears,
  But all would not prevail.

Their bodies, bath'd in purple blood,
  They bore with them away ;
They kiss'd them dead a thousand times,
  When they were clad in clay.

This news was brought to Edinburgh,
  Where Scotland's king did reign,
That brave earl Douglas suddenly
  Was with an arrow slain.

O heavy news ! king James did say,
  Scotland can witness be,
I have not any captain more
  Of such account as he.

Like tidings to king Henry came,
　Within as short a space,
That Percy of Northumberland
　Was slain in Chevy-chase.

Now God be with him ! said our king,
　Sith 'twill no better be ;
I trust I have within my realm
　Five hundred as good as he.

Yet shall no Scot nor Scotland say,
　But I will vengeance take ;
And be revenged on them all,
　For brave Lord Percy's sake.

This vow full well the king perform'd,
　After on Humble-down :
In one day fifty knights were slain,
　With lords of great renown ;

And of the rest, of small account,
　Did many hundreds die.
Thus ended the hunting of Chevy-chase,
　Made by the earl Percy.

God save the king, and bless the land
　In plenty, joy, and peace ;
And grant, henceforth, that foul debate
　'Twixt noblemen may cease.

Fair 'Mabel' of Wallington.

WHEN we were silly sisters seven, sisters [we] were so fair,

Five of us were brave knights wives, and died in child-bed fair.

Up then spake fair 'Mabel,' marry wou'd she nane,

If ever she came in man's bed the same gate wad she gang.

Make no vows, fair 'Mabel,' for fear they broken be,

Here's been the knight of Wallington, asking good-will of thee.

Here's been the knight [of Wallington], mother, asking good-will of me;

Within three-quarters of a year, you may come bury me.

When she came to Wallington, and into Wallington-hall,

There she spy'd her mother dear walking about the wall.

You're welcome, daughter dear, to thy castle and
thy bower.
I thank you kindly, mother, I hope they'll soon
be your's.
She had not been in Wallington three-quarters
and a day,
Till upon the ground she could not walk, she was
a weary prey ;
She had not been in Wallington three-quarters
and a night,
Till on the ground she cou'd not walk, she was a
weary ' wight.'

Is there ne'er a boy in this town who'll win hose
and shun,
That will run to fair Pudlington, and bid my
mother come ?
Up then spake a little boy, near unto [her] a-kin,
Full oft I have your errands gone, but now I will
it run.
Then she call'd her waiting-maid to bring up
bread and wine :
Eat and drink my bonny boy, thou'll ne'er eat
more of mine :
Give my respects to my mother, as [she] ' sits ' in
her chair of stone,
And ask her how she likes the news of seven to
have but one.

Give my love to my brother William, Ralph, and
    John ;
And to my sister Betty fair, and to her white as
    bone,
And bid her keep her maidenhead, be sure make
    much on't,
For if e'er she come in man's bed the same gate
    will she gang.
Away this little boy is gone as fast as he could run,
When he came where brigs were broke he lay
    down and 'swum.'
When he saw the lady, he said, Lord may your
    keeper be !
What news, my pretty boy, 'hast' thou to tell
    to me ?

Your daughter ' Mabel ' orders me, as you sit in a
    chair of stone,
To ask you how you like the news of seven to
    have but one ;
Your daughter gives commands as you sit in a
    chair of ' state.'
And bids you come to her sickening, her ' weary '
    lake-wake :
She gives command to her brother William, Ralph,
    and John ;
To her sister Betty fair, and to her white [as]
    bone,

She bids her keep her maidenhead, besure make
    much on't,
For if e'er she come in man's bed the same gate
    wou'd she gang.

She kickt the table with her foot, she kickt it
    with her knee,
The silver plate into the fire so far she made it
    flee :
Then she call'd her waiting-maid to bring her
    riding-hood,
So did she on her stable-groom to bring her ' steed
    so good : '
Go saddle to me the black, go saddle to me the
    brown,
Go saddle to me the swiftest steed that e'er rid
    Wallington.
When she came to Wallington, and into Walling-
    ton-hall,
There she espy'd her son Fenwick walking about
    the wall.

God save you, dear son, Lord may your keeper
    be !
Where is my daughter fair, that used to walk with
    thee ?
He turn'd his head round about, the tears did fill
    his eye ;
'Tis a month, he said, since she took her chambers
    from me.

She went on, and there were in the hall
Four and twenty ladies letting the tears down fall :
IIer daughter had a scope into her chest, and into
    her chin,
All to keep her life till her dear mother came.

Come take the rings off my finger, the skin it is
    [so] white,
And give them to my mother dear, for she was all
    the ' weight ; '
Come take the rings off my fingers, the veins are
    so red,
Give them to sir William Fenwick, I'm sure his
    heart will bleed.
She took out a razor, that was both sharp and fine,
And out of her left side has taken the heir of
    Wallington.
There is a race in Wallington, and that I rue full
    sare,
Tho' the cradle it be full spread up, the bride-bed
    is left bare.

SONG V.

A lamentable Ditty, made upon the death of a worthy gentleman, named GEORGE STOOLE, *dwelling sometime on Gate-side Moor, and some time at Newcastle, in Northumberland: with his penitent end.* [c. 1610.]

To a delicate Scottish Tune.

COME you lusty Northerne lads,
　That are so blith and bonny,
Prepare your hearts to be full sad,
　To heare the end of Georgy.
　　Heigh-ho, heigh-ho my bonny love,
　　Heigh-ho, heigh-ho my honny;
　　Heigh-ho, heigh-ho my owne dear love,
　　And God be with my Georgie.

When Georgie to his triall came,
　A thousand hearts were sorry,
A thousand lasses wept full sore,
　And all for love of Georgie.
　　Heigh-ho, heigh-ho my bonny love,
　　Heigh-ho, &c.
Z

Some did say he would escape,
  Some at his fall did glory:
But these were clownes and fickle friends,
  And none that loved Georgy.
        Heigh-ho, &c.

Might friends have satisfide the law,
  Then G[e]orgie would find many :
Yet bravely did he plead for life,
  If mercy might be any.
        Heigh-ho, &c.

But when this doughty carle was cast,
  He was full sad and sorry :
Yet boldly did he take his death,
  So patiently dyde Georgie.
        Heigh-ho, &c.

As Georgie went up to the gate,
  He tooke his leave of many :
He tooke his leave of his lards wife,
  Whom he lov'd best of any.
        Heigh-ho, &c.

With thousand sighs and heavy looks,
  Away from thence he parted,
Where he so often blithe had beene,
  Though now so heavy hearted.
        Heigh-ho, &c.

He writ a letter with his owne hand,
  He thought he writ it bravely :
He sent it to New-castle towne,
  To his beloved lady.
      Heigh-ho, &c.

Wherein he did at large bewaile,
  The occasion of his folly ;
Bequeathing life unto the law,
  His soule to heaven holy.
      Heigh-ho, &c.

Why, lady, leave to weepe for me,
  Let not my ending grieve ye :
Prove constant to the ' man ' you love,
  For I cannot releeve yee.
      Heigh-ho, &c.

Out upon the, Withrington,
  And fie upon the, Phœnix :
Thou hast put downe the doughty one
  That stole the sheepe trom Anix.
      [Heigh-ho, &c.]

And fie on all such cruell carles,
  Whose crueltie's so fickle,
To cast away a gentleman
  In hatred for so little.
      Heigh-ho, &c.

I would I were on yonder hill,
  Where I have beene full merry :
My sword and buckeler by my side
  To fight till I be weary.
      Heigh-ho, &c.

They well should know that tooke me first
  Though whoops be now forsaken :
Had I but freedome, armes, and health,
  I'de dye are I'de be taken.
      Heigh-ho, &c.

But law condemns me to my grave,
  They have me in their power ;
Ther's none but Christ that can me save,
  At this my dying houre.
      Heigh-ho, &c.

He call'd his dearest love to him,
  When as his heart was sorry :
And speaking thus with manly heart,
  Deare sweeting, pray for Georgie.
      Heigh-ho, &c.

He gave to her a piece of gold,
  And bade her givet't her barnes :
And oft he kist her rosie lips,
  And laid him into her armes.
      Heigh-ho, &c.

And coming to the place of death,
  He never changed colour,
The more they thought he would look pale,
  The more his veines were fuller.
      Heigh-ho, &c.

And with a cheerefull countenance,
  (Being at that time entreated
For to confesse his former life)
  These words he straight repeated.
      Heigh-ho, &c.

I never stole no oxe nor cow,
  Nor never murdered any :
But fifty horse I did receive
  Of a merchants man of Gory.
      Heigh-ho, &c.

For which I am condemn'd to dye
  Though guiltlesse I stand dying :
Deare gracious God, my soule receive,
  For now my life is flying.
      Heigh-ho, &c.

The man of death a part did act,
  Which grieves me tell the story ;
God comfort all are comfortlesse,
  And did so well as Georgie.
    Heigh-ho, heigh-ho, my bonny love,
      Heigh-ho, heigh-[ho] my bonny ;
    Heigh-ho, heigh-ho, mine own true love,
      Sweet Christ receive my Georgie.

SONG VI.

AN EXCELLENT BALLAD OF

THE SICKNESS, DEATH, AND BURIAL,

OF ECKYS MARE.

*Which was made and composed by the late ancient
and famous Northern poet,* MR. BERNARD
RUMNEY, *a musician, or country fidler, who
lived and died at Rothbury, being about one
hundred years old at the time of his death.*

WOLD you please to heare of a sang of dule,
  Of yea sad chance and pittifow case,
Makes the peur man powt through mony a pule,
  And leuk on mony an unkenned face?

Between the Yule but and the Pasch,
  In a private place, where as I lay,
I heard ane sigh, and cry, Alas!
  What shall I outher dea or say?

A man that's born of a middle-yeard wight,
  For wealth or pelth can no be secure;
For he may have enough at night,
  And the next morn he may be fow peur.

I speak this by a Northumberland man,
    The proverb's true proves by himself;
Since in horse-couping he began,
    He had great cause to crack of wealth.

Of galloways he was well stockt,
    With some part first, with some part last;
But I'll no speak much to his praise,
    For some of them gat o're lang a fast.

Some of them gat a shrowish cast,
    Which was nea teaken of much pelth;
But yet he hopes, if life dea last,
    To see the day to crack of welth.

But aye the warst cast still comes last,
    He had nea geud left but a Mear,
There was mea diseases did her attend
    Nor I can name in half a year.

If Markham he himself was here,
    A famous farrier although he be,
It wad set aw his wits astear
    To reckon her diseases in their degree.

But her sicknesses we'll set aside,
    Now tauk we of the peur mans cost,
And how she lev'd, and how she dead,
    And how his labour aw was lost.

In the winter-time she took a hoast,
  And aw whilk while she was noe weell;
But yet her stomach ne're was lost,
  Although she never had her heal.

Now for her feud she went so yare,
  An the fiend had been a truss of hey,
She wad a swallowed him and mickle mare,
  Bequeen the night ' but ' an the dey.

The peur man cries out Armyes aye,
  I see that she's noe like to mend,
She beggars me with haver and hey,
  I wish her some untimeous end.

Nea sooner pray'd but as soon heard,
  She touck a fawing down behind,
She wad a thousand men a scar'd,
  To have felt her how she fil'd the wind.

Her master he went out at night,
  Of whilk he had oft mickle need,
He left her neane her bed to right,
  Nor neane for to had up her head.

Next day when he came to the town,
  He ran to see his mear with speed,
He thought she had fawn in a swoon,
  But when he try'd she was cald dead.

It's ever alas ! but what remeed,
  Had she play'd me this at Michaelmas,
It wad a studden me in geud steed,
  And sav'd me both yeats, hay and grass.

There's ne'er an elf in aw the town,
  That hardly we'll can say his creed,
But he will swear a solemn oath,
  Crack o'wealth Eckys mear cau'd dead.

Lad, wilt thou for Hob Trumble run ?
  I ken he will come at my need ;
That seun he may take off her skin,
  For I maun leeve though she be dead.

Now straight he came with knife in hand,
  He flead her fra the top to th' tail,
He left nea mare skin on her aw
  Then wad been a hunden to a flail.

He seld her haill hide for a groat,
  So far I let you understand,
And what he did weed he may well weet,
  For he bought neither house nor land.

Now have I cassen away my care,
  And hope to live to get another ;
And night and day shall be my prayer,
  The fiend gea down the loaning with her.

Now shall I draw it near an end,
  And tauk nea mare of her at least,
But hoping none for to offend,
  You shall hear part of her funeral feast.

To her resorted mony a beak,
  And birds of sundry sorts of hue ;
There was three hundred at the least,
  You may believe it to be true.

Sir Ingrim Corby he came first there,
  With his fair lady clad in black,
And with him swarms there did appear
  Of piots hoping at his back.

The carrion craw she was not slack,
  Aw cled into her mourning weed,
With her resorted mony a mack
  Of greedy kite and hungry gleede.

When they were aw conven'd compleat,
  And every yean had taen their place ;
So rudely they fell tea their meat,
  But nane thought on to say the grace.

Some rip'd her ribs, some pluck'd her face,
  Nea bit of her was to be seen ;
Sir Ingrim Corby in that place,
  Himself he pick'd out baith her eyne.

But wait ye what an a chance befel,
  When they were at this jolly chear,
Sir William Bark, I can you tell,
  He unexpected lighted there.

Put aw the feasters in sike a fear,
  Some hopt away, some flew aside,
There was not ane durst come him near,
  Nay not sir Corby, nor his bride.

He came not with a single side,
  For mony a tike did him attend,
I wait he was no puft wea pride,
  As you shall hear before I end.

See rudely they fell to the meat,
  But napkin, trencher, salt, or knife;
Some to the head, some to the feet,
  Whiles banes geud bare there was na strife.

In came there a tike, they cau'd him Grim,
  Sea greedily he did her gripe,
But he rave out her belly-rim,
  And aw her puddings he made pipe.

Her lights, her liver, but an her tripe,
  They all lay trailing upon the green;
They were aw gane with a sudden wipe,
  Not any of them was to be seen.

But suddenly begeud a feast,
 And after that begeud a fray ;
The tikes that were baith weak and least,
 They carried aw the bats away.

And they that were of the weaker sort,
 They harl'd her through the paddock-peul,
They leugh, and said it was geud sport,
 When they had drest her like a feule.

Thus have you heard of Ekies mear,
 How pitifully she made her end ;
I write unto you far and near,
 Who says her death is no well penn'd,

I leave it to yoursel's to mend
 That chance the peur man need again ;
If it be ill penn'd it is as well kend,
 I got as little for my ‘pain.’

PART II.

TABLE OF CONTENTS.

VII. The Midford Galloways Ramble . 193

VIII. The Insipids : or, The Mistress with
her Multitude of Man Servants . 201

IX. Sawney Ogilby's Duel with his Wife 206

X. The Felton Garland . . . 209

XI. The Laidley Worm of Spindleston-
Heugh 216

XII. On the First Rebellion . . . 224

XIII. The Colliers Rant 227

XIV. Weel may the Keel Row . . 229

XV. Bonny Keel Laddie . . . 230

XVI. Newcastle Beer . . . 231

Ｔhe Ｍidford Ｇalloway's Ramble.

By THOMAS WHITTEL.

To the Tune of *Ranting roaring Willy.*

THE routing the earl of Mar's forces,
 Has given their neighbours supplies ;
They've stock'd us with Highlanders horses,
 Like kileys for madness and size :
The whirligig-maker of Midford
 Has gotten one holds such a stear,
He's had worse work with it, I'll say for't
 Than Ecky e'er had with his mare.

The devil ne'er saw such a gelding
 As this to be fol'd of a mear ;
The size ont's a shame to be teld on,
 And yet it could skip like a deer ;
For colour and size (I'm a sinner,
 I scorn, as the folks says, to slide,)
'Twas just like Hob Trumble's gimmer,
 Which he sold for six-pence a side.

It was a confounded bad liver,
   Like Ferry the piper's old cat ;
It ne'er could be brought to behaviour,
   Though it has got many a bat :
It had been so spoil'd in up-bringing,
   It vext his poor heart ev'ry day ;
Sometimes with biting and flinging,
   And sometimes with running away.

Perhaps it was brought up a Tory,
   And knew the poor man for a Whig :
But for to make short a long story,
   I'll tell you one day what it did :
When business came thicker and thicker,
   And would not admit of delay,
As fast as the heels on't could bicker,
   It scamper'd on northward away.

O'er rocks, over mountains and ditches,
   Dike-gutters and hedges it speals ;
A courser could never keep stretches
   With it for a large share of heels :
From hill unto dale like a farie,
   It hurry'd and pranced along,
While Geordy was in a quandary,
   And knew not what way ' it' was gone.

A day or two after, have at it,
   He north in pursuit on't took chase,
And like a dub-skelper he troted,
   To many [a] strange village and place :

All Rothbury forest he ranged,
    From corner to corner like mad,
And still he admired and stranged,
    What vengeance was gone with his pad.

He circuled about like a ring-worm,
    And follow'd the scent of his nose,
And from Heslyhurst unto Brinkburn,
    With Fortune the clothier he goes.
To honest Tom Fawdon's the fuller,
    The rattle-brain'd roisters both went,
Tho' they made the gelding their colour,
    Another thing was their intent.

Tom Fawdon soon knew what they wanted,
    And straightway the table was set,
With bread, butter and cheese it was planted,
    And good ale, as well as good meat ;
Their grace took but little inditing,
    'Twas short and they had it by heart,
And they took as little inviting,
    But strove who should have the fore-start.

They used no bashful dissembling,
    But to in a passion did fall,
The dishes did by them stand trembling,
    Their mercy appeared so small :
The butter, the cheese, and the bannocks,
    Disolved like snow in a fresh,
And still as they stuck in their stomachs,
    With liquor they did them down wash.

The Dutch, nor the Welsh, nor wight Wallace,
  Did ever like them show their spleen,
The cheese bore the marks of their malice,
  Their knives and their teeth were so keen.
Two stone they destroyed, shame be'n them,
  And pour'd down their liquor like spouts,
Their guts to hold what they put in them,
  Were dressed like a pair of strait boots.

With bellies top-full to the rigging,
  I leave them to settle a bit,
Till making good use of the midding,
  ' Do ' bring them unto a right set.
Now come we to speak of the gelding,
  Who knowing that he did offend,
Stay'd two or three days about Weldon,
  To make justice Lisle stand his friend.

He after that grew so unlucky,
  On mischief and ill he was bent,
He prov'd a right North-country jockey,
  Still cheating where ever he went.
At many mens charges he dined,
  But never ask'd what was arrear ;
Yet no man could get him confined,
  So slily himself he did clear.

The town of Longframlington further
  Can give an account what he is,
He came within acting of murder,
  As near as a horse could to miss ;

For into a house he went scudding,
   And seeing a child all alone,
If Providence had not withstood him,
   He'd struck it as dead as a stone.

The rest of his acts are recorded,
   'Tis nonsence to mention them here ;
I'll go back and fetch Geordy forward,
   He's tarri'd too long I do fear !
From Brinkburn he started and held on,
   Directly to Framlington town,
And then to the miller's at Weldon,
   He back o'er the hill tumbled down.

Not finding the thing that he wanted,
   Unto Hedlowood he did trot,
He was tossed like a dog in a blanket,
   O'er Cocket and back in a boat :
All Framlington fields he sought over,
   And from spot to spot he did run,
For fear the grass chanced to cover
   His pad, as it once did Tom Thumb.

Then up to John Alders he drabbeth,
   And there all the night did repose,
And then, the next day being Sabbath,
   Away he to Whittingham goes ;
Where he to revenge the miscarriage
   Of his little scatter-brain'd nag,
He went to the clerk of the parish,
   To get him expos'd for a vague.

The clerk he soon set up his cropping,
    And made a great bustle and stear ;
The church-yard appear'd like a hopping,
    The folks drew about so to hear :
He did to a hairs-breadth describe him,
    And call'd him again and again,
And Geordy by four-pence did bribe him,
    For all the small pains he had ta'n.

Scarce were the jawbones of these asses
    Well shut, till a Thranton-bred lad,
Eas'd Geordy a bit of his crosses,
    By bringing some news of his pad :
These tidings his spirit renewed,
    No clerk cou'd his courage controul,
But still was resolv'd to pursue it,
    Suppose it were to the North pole.

'Tis past a man's giving account on,
    What way he traversed with speed,
From Eslington, Whittingham, Thranton,
    He past the Broom-park and Hill-head,
To Leirchil, to Barton, to Branton,
    And from thence to mount on the clay,
To Fawdon, the Clinch, and to Glanton,
    And several towns mist by the way.

There's Lemendon, Allerwick, Bolton,
    With Woodhall that stands on the fell,
And Titlington's likewise untold on,
    Where Jacob, of old, dig'd his well ;

To Harup, to Hidgily and Beenly,
　He past unto Galloway mill,
To Brandon, to Ingrom, and Revely,
　And Crowly that stands on a hill.

To Brandon-main, then to the Whitehouse,
　To Dickison's, where he made a league,
And articled that for a night-house,
　To rest a while after fatigue :
He drank a while till he grew mellow,
　And then for his chamber did call,
Where sound he may sleep, silly fellow,
　His travels wou'd weary us all.

He had an invincible couple
　Of legs, that did bear him well out,
They hung so loose, like a flail-souple,
　And cudgel'd his buttocks about ;
No man wou'd have thought any hallion
　Could ever have acted the thing,
Without help of Pacolet's stallion,*
That when the pin turn'd did take wing.

Next day rising, rigging and starting,
　He jogg'd on his journey with speed,
To Bewick, the Lilburns, Culdmartin,
　From thence unto Woolerhaugh-head ;

---

* See the history of Valentine and Orson.

To Wopperton, Ilderton, Rodham,
　And Rosdon, he scudded like mad,
Nothing fell by the way that withstood him,
　Until he had met with his pad.

Earl was the place where he found him,
　A blithe sight for Geordy to see ;
But got the whole town to surround him,
　Before he his prisoner would be :
Then on his back jumping and prancing,
　He swiftly switcht over the plain,
But made him pay dear for his dancing,
　E'er he got to Midford again.

SONG VIII.

THE INSIPIDS:

OR,

The Mistress with her Multitude of Man Servants.

BY THE SAME AUTHOR.

OF all the Kirkharle bonny lasses,
  If they were set round in a ring,
Jane Heymours for beauty surpasses,
  She might be a match for a king;
Her cheeks are as red as a cherry,
  Her breast is as white as a swan,
She is a blyth lass and a merry,
  And her middle is fit for a man.

The lads are so fond to be at her,
  They run all as mad as March hares,
This bonny young lass they do flatter,
  And fall at her feet to their prayers;
You never saw keener or stouter,
  They'll not be put off with delay,
Like bull-doggs they still hang about her,
  And court her by night and by day.

Jo Hepple, Will Crudders, Tom Liddle,
　With twenty or thirty men more,
If I could their names but unriddle,
　At least I might make out two score.
That all cast about for to catch her,
　And make her their own during life;
With others that strive to debauch her,
　Despairing to make her their wife.

So many love tokens and fancies
　She gets, that to bring them in view,
They'd look like so many romances,
　And none could believe they were true.
I only will mention one favour,
　And leave you to guess at the rest;
An old kenning Edward Hall gave her,
　Of comforts the choicest and best.

They venture like people for prizes,
　And with the same timorous doubt,
She has them of all sorts and sizes,
　That's constantly sneaking about.
Each man speaks her fair, and importunes
　In all the best language that's known;
And happy were he could tell fortunes,
　To know if the girl were his own.

John Robson, Jo Bowman, Will Little,
　With her would spend night's over days;
Each glance of her eyes is so smittle,
　That all men are catch'd if they gaze:

She strikes them quite thro' with love stitches,
    And many [a] poor heart she doth fill ;
She's like one of those call'd white witches,
    That hurts men and means them no ill.

John Henderson, that honest weaver,
    And metled Matt Thomson the smith,
Came both from Capheaton to preave her,
    And court her with courage and pith.
Ned Oliver too, and Tom Baxter
    Spare neither their feet, tongue, or hands,
But strive with the rest to contract her
    In compass of conjugal bands.

Bob Bewick just makes it his calling
    Unto her his love to declare ;
And some's of that mind that John Rawling
    Would gladly come in for a share.
John Forcing doth praise and commend her,
    Above any lass that wears head ;
And fain he would be a pretender,
    If he had but hopes to come speed.

Bob Cole strains his wit and invention
    And compliments to a degree ;
And twenty that I cannot mention
    Are all as keen courters as he.
She puts them all into such pickle
    They care not what courses they run,
And if (as folk says) she be fickle,
    'Tis twenty to one they're undone.

Their loves would fill forty hand wallets,
  If they were cramm'd in at both ends ;
Their hearts are all sunk like lead pellets,
  And very small hopes of amends.
Great dangers on both sides encreases,
  Which very destructive may prove ;
The lass may be all pull'd to pieces,
  Or all the poor lads die for love.

But that which supports and preserves them,
  Their stomachs their best friends do prove ;
And 'tis not a little meat serves them
  Since they fell so deeply in love.
Their fancies and appetites working,
  It made them so sharp and so keen,
The girls mother lost two butter firkins,
  They wattell'd away so much cream.

One day with a good brandy bottle,
  Two met her about the Heugh Nebb,
And there their accounts they did settle,
  And made all as right as my legg :
The snuff-mill and gloves came in season,
  The want of a glass to supply ;
They drank the girls first, with good reason,
  And then the kings health by the by.

The Millers Haugh, Heugh Nebb, and Haystack,
  The Flowers, the New Close, and Decoy,
With places whose titles I know not,
  Where they met to love and enjoy,

Would be but too far a digression,
　And make our fond passions rebell;
But, oh! had these places expression,
　What pretty love tales they could tell!

So many to her bear affection,
　And give her such lofty applause,
I'm love-sick to hear the description,
　And wish I could see the sweet cause:
'Tis she that could make all odds even,
　And bring many wonders to pass;
I wish all her sweethearts in heaven,
　While I were in bed with the lass!

SONG IX.

Sawney Ogilby's Duel with his Wife.

BY THE SAME AUTHOR.

To the Tune of *The Worst's past.*

GOOD people, give ear to the fatalest duel
  That Morpeth e'er saw since it was a town,
Where fire is kindled and has so much fuel,
    I wou'd not be [he] that wou'd quench't for a
    crown.
Poor Sawney, as canny a North British hallion,
  As e'er crost the border this million of weeks,
Miscarried, and married a Scottish tarpawlin,
    That pays his pack-shoulders, and will have
    the breeks.

I pity him still when I think of his kindred,
  Lord Ogleby was his near cousin of late ;
And if he and somebody else had not hinder'd,
  He might have been heir unto all his estate.

His stature was small, and his shape like a
    monkey,
  His beard like a bundle of scallions or leeks ;
Right bonny he was, but now he's worn scrunty,
  And fully as fit for the horns as the breeks.

It fell on a day, he may it remember,
  Tho' others rejoyced, yet so did not he,
When tidings was brought that Lisle did surrender,
  It grieves me to think on't, his wife took the gee.
These bitches still itches, and stretches commission,
  And if they be crossed they're still taking peeks,
And Sawney, poor man, he was out of condition,
And hardly well fit for defending the breeks.

She mutter'd, and moung'd, and looked damn'd
    misty,
  And Sawney said something, as who cou'd for-
    bear ?
Then straight she began, and went to't handyfisty,
  She wither'd about, and dang down all the gear :
The dishes and dublers went flying like fury,
  She broke more that day than would mend in
    two weeks,
And had it been put to a judge or a jury,
They cou'd not tell whether deserved the breeks.

But Sawney grew weary, and fain would been civil,
  Being ald, and unfeary, and fail'd of his strength,
Then she cowp'd him o'er the kale-pot with a kevil,
  And there he lay labouring all his long length.

His body was soddy, and sore he was bruised,
　The bark of his shins was all standing in peaks ;
No stivet e'er lived was so much misused
　As sarey ald Sawney for claiming the breeks.

The noise was so great all the neighbours did
　　hear them,
　She made his scalp ring like the clap of a bell ;
But never a soul had the mense to come near
　　them,
　Tho' he shouted murder with many a yell.
She laid on whisky whasky, and held like a steary,
　Wight Wallace could hardly have with her kept
　　steaks ;
And never gave over until she was weary,
　And Sawney was willing to yield her the breeks.

And now she must still be observ'd like a madam,
　She'll cause him to curvet, and skip like a frogg,
And if he refuses she's ready to scad him,
　Poxtake such a life, it wou'd weary a dogg.
Ere I were so serv'd, I would see the de'il take
　　her
　I hate both the name and the nature of sneaks ;
But if she were mine I would clearly forsake her,
　And let her make a kirk and a mill of the
　　breeks.

SONG X.

The Felton Garland.

How a Brick-maker at Felton stole a young
woman away, by her own consent,
from her grandmother.

To the Tune of Maggy Lawther, &c.

THERE lives a lass in Felton town,
　Her name is Jen—y Gow—n,
With the Brick-man she has played the lown,
　So wanton she is grown :
The reason why some love the night,
　Incognito to revel,
Is they love darkness more than light,
　Because their deeds are evil.

So late at night on Saturday,
　He thought all safe as brandy,
He rigg'd and trigg'd, and rid away
　Upon John Hinks's Sandy :
To Haggerston he did pretend,
　Some sweetheart there confin'd him ;
But he took up, at our town-end,
　His cloak-bag on behind him.

Like as the bird that gay would be,
  As fable hath reported,
From each fine bird most cunningly
  A feather she extorted :
Then boasting said, How fine I'm grown
  Her painted plumes she shaked,
At which each bird pluck'd off their own,
  And left her almost naked.

With this kind maid it proved so,
  Who many things did borrow,
To rig her up from toe to toe,
  And deck her like Queen Flora.
Of one she got a black-silk hood,
  Her fond light head to cover,
Likewise a blue cloak, very good,
  Her night intreagues to smother.

Clock stockings she must have (dear wot)
  In borrow'd shoes she's kilted,
Some lent her a blue petticoat,
  Both large and bravely quilted.
Of some she got a fine linn-smock,
  Lest Pet—r shou'd grow canty,
And have a stroke at her black joak,
  With a tante, rante, tante.

With a borrow'd cane, hat on her head,
  To make her still look greater,
She'd make her friends believe indeed,
  They were all bought by Pet—er.

But when she did return again,
 In all her boasted grandeur,
Each to 'their' own did lay just claim,
 And left her as they fand her.

But none can guess at 'their' intent,
 Why they abroad did swagger,
Some said, to see 'their' friends they went,
 Some said, to Buckle Beggar.
Away full four days they stay'd,
 I think they took 'their' leisure,
They past for man and wife, some said,
 And spent the nights in pleasure.

When the Black Cock did his Sandy see
 There was a joyful meeting,
That night when I thee lent, quoth he,
 I wish I had been sleeping :
Thou art abused very sore,
 As any creature can be,
And still he cry'd o'er and o'er,
 O woe is me for Sandy !

Then Sandy, mumbling, made reply,
 You were my loving master,
I never did your suit deny,
 Nor meet with one disaster,
Till now unknown to your self,
 That I shou'd had this trouble,
Or else for neither love nor pelf,
 You'd let me carry double.

Poor Sandy was with riding daul'd,
   He rues he saw their faces,
His back and sides they sorely gaul'd,
   He pay'd for their embraces ;
But if young Pet—r's found her nest,
   She'll rue as well as Sandy,
And if she proves with child, she best
   Had tarry'd with her grandy.

How they abused the horse they rid on, and when
married, they went off in several people's debts.

In second part I will declare
   The troubles of poor Sandy ;
And how this couple married were,
   And how well pleas'd was Grandy.
Now first with Sandy I'll begin,
   Whose leggs swell'd to a wonder,'
So likewise was his belly rim,
   Swell'd like to burst asunder.

And lest his troubles shou'd increase,
   A farrier was provided,
Well skill'd in Markham's master-piece,
   Who in this town resided ;
And, to his everlasting fame,
   He did exert his cunning,
He bled his leggs, and in his waim,
   Two tapps he there sets running.

He several medicines did apply,
   Whose vertue was so pure,
That in six weeks, or very nigh,
   He made a perfect cure.
And now in all the world besides,
   There's rot a sounder creature,
So well he scampers, and he rides,
   But never more with Pet—r.

Of him I now design to speak
   A Yorkshire born and bred, sir,
He play'd them all a Yorkshire trick,
   And then away he fled, sir,
As you shall hear when home he came,
   With Jennet upon Sandy,
He to his work return'd again,
   And she unto her grandy.

But long with her she tarry'd not,
   Unsettled was her notion,
Just like the pend'lum of a clock,
   That's always in a motion.
I'll go to service, she did say,
   Keep me, you cannot afford it ;
So one she got, where was it, pray ?
   E'en where her spark was boarded.

Now whether 'twas for want of beds,
   Or whether it was cold weather,
Or whether 'twas to measure legs,
   That they lay both together ;

But they smuggl'd for a while,
    And gave out they were marry'd,
Till she at length did prove with child,
    Then all things were miscarry'd.

Then he did own his fault was great,
    He'd make her satisfaction,
And fearing penance ' in ' a ' sheet,'
    He'd suffer for that action,
He'd marry her without delay,
    And got ' their ' nuptial lesson,
Which to confirm they went streightway
    To get their grandy's blessing.

When in her presence they were come,
    She rail'd at them like thunder,
For shame, cries she, what have you done,
    That's brought you on this blunder?
She call'd her slut and brazen faced,
    Instead of kind caressing,
Our family you have disgrac'd,
    Can you expect a blessing?

But like a stormy winter's night,
    Next morning turns calm weather,
So grandy's passion soon took flight,
    She pray'd that they together
Might live in love and happiness,
    Enjoying peace and plenty,
Long may they health and wealth possess,
    And pockets ne'er grow empty.

When they had grandy's blessing got,
  They slyly fled away, sir,
He all the bricks did leave unwrought,
  And many debts to pay, sir.
Now all good people warning take,
  How you do trust to strangers,
They'll wheadle you for money sake,
  And still prove country rangers.

THE LAIDLEY WORM

Of Spindleston-Heugh.

Virgo jam serpens sinuosa volumina versat,
Mille trahens varios adverso sole colores,
Arrectis horret squamis et sibilat ore ;
Arduaque insurgens navem de littore pulsat.

A song above 500 years old, made by the old
mountain-bard, Duncan Frasier, living on
Cheviot, A.D. 1270.

Printed from an antient manuscript.

(BY MR. ROBERT LAMBE, VICAR OF NORHAM.)

THE king is gone from Bambrough Castle,
   Long may the princess mourn,
Long may she stand on the castle wall,
   Looking for his return.

She has knotted the keys upon a string,
   And with her she has them ta'en,
She has cast them o'er her left shoulder,
   And to the gate she is gane.

She tripped out, she tripped in,
  She tript into the yard ;
But it was more for the king's sake
  Than for the queen's regard.

It fell out on a day, the king
  Brought the queen with him home ;
And all the lords, in our country,
  To welcome them did come.

Oh ! welcome father, the lady cries,
  Unto your halls and bowers ;
And so are you, my step-mother,
  For all that's here is yours.

A lord said, wondering while she spake,
  This princess of the North
Surpasses all of female kind
  In beauty, and in worth.

The envious queen replied, At least,
  You might have excepted me ;
In a few hours, I will her bring
  Down to a low degree.

I will her liken to a Laidley worm,
  That warps about the stone,
And not, till childy Wynd comes back,
  Shall she again be won.

The princess stood at the bower door
  Laughing, who could her blame?
But e'er the next day's sun went down,
  A long worm she became.

For seven miles east, and seven miles west,
  And seven miles north, and south,
No blade of grass or corn could grow,
  So venomous was her mouth.

The milk of seven stately cows,
  It was costly her to keep,
Was brought her daily, which she drank
  Before she went to sleep.

At this day may be seen the cave,
  Which held her folded up,
And the stone trough, the very same
  Out of which she did sup.

Word went east, and word went west,
  And word is gone over the sea,
That a Laidley worm in Spindleston-Heughs
  Would ruin the North Country.

Word went east, and word went west,
  And over the sea did go;
The child of Wynd got wit of it,
  Which filled his heart with woe.

He called straight his merry men all,
    They thirty were and three :
I wish I were at Spindleston,
    This desperate worm to see.

We have no time now here to waste,
    Hence quickly let us sail :
My only sister Margaret,
    Something, I fear, doth ail.

They built a ship without delay,
    With masts of the rown tree,
With flutring sails of silk so fine,
    And set her on the sea.

They went on board.   The wind with speed,
    Blew them along the deep,
At length they spied an huge square tower
    On a rock high and steep.

The sea was smooth, the weather clear,
    When they approached nigher,
King Ida's castle they well knew,
    And the banks of Bambroughshire.

The Queen look'd out at her bow window,
    To see what she could see ;
There she espied a gallant ship
    Sailing upon the sea.

When she beheld the silken sails,
  Full glancing in the sun,
To sink the ship she went away,
  Her witch wives every one.

The spells were vain ; the hags returned
  To the queen in sorrowful mood,
Crying that witches have no power,
  Where there is rown-tree wood.

Her last effort, she sent a boat,
  Which in the haven lay,
With armed men to board the ship.
  But they were driven away.

The worm lept out, the worm lept down,
  She plaited round the stone ;
And ay as the ship came to the land
  She banged it off again.

The child then ran out of her reach
  The ship on Budley-sand ;
And jumping into the shallow sea,
  Securely got to land.

And now he drew his berry-broad sword,
  And laid it on her head ;
And swore if she did harm to him
  That he would strike her dead.

O ! quit thy sword and bend thy bow,
  And give me kisses three ;
For though I am a poisonous worm,
  No hurt I'll do to thee.

Oh ! quit thy sword, and bend thy bow,
  And give me kisses three ;
If I'm not won, e're the sun go down,
  Won I shall never be.

He quitted his sword and bent his bow,
  He gave her kisses three ;
She crept into a hole a worm,
  But out stept a lady.

No cloathing had this lady fine,
  To keep her from the cold,
He took his mantle from him about,
  And round her did it fold.

He has taken his mantle from him about,
  And in it he wrapt her in,
And they are up to Bambrough castle,
  As fast as they can win.

His absence and her serpent shape,
  The King had long deplored,
He now rejoyced to see them both
  Again to him restored.

The queen they wanted, whom they found
 All pale, and sore afraid ;
Because she knew her power must yield
 To Childy Wynds, who said,

Woe be to thee, thou wicked witch,
 An ill death mayest thou dee ;
As thou my sister hast lik'ned,
 So lik'ned shalt thou be.

I will turn you into a toad,
 That on the ground doth wend ;
And won, won, shalt thou never be,
 Till this world hath an end.

Now on the sand near Ida's tower,
 She crawls a loathsome toad,
And venom spits on every maid
 She meets upon her road.

The virgins all of Bambrough town
 Will swear that they have seen
This spiteful toad, of monstrous size,
 Whilst walking they have been.

All folks believe within the shire
 This story to be true,
And they all run to Spindleston,
 The cave and trough to view.

This fact now Duncan Frasier
Of Cheviot, sings in rhime ;
Lest Bambrough-shire-men should forge
Some part of it in time.

SONG XII.

On the First Rebellion.

MACKINTOSH was a soldier brave,
And of his friends he took his leave,
Towards Northumberland he drew,
Marching along with ' a' jovial crew.

The lord Derwentwater he did say,
Five hundred guineas he would lay,
To fight the militia, if they would stay,
But they prov'd cowards and ran away.

The earl of Mar did vow and swear,
That if e'er proud Preston he did come near,
Before the right should starve and the wrong stand,
He'd blow them into some foreign land.

The lord Derwentwater he did say,
When he mounted on his dapple grey,
I wish that we were at home with speed,
For I fear we are all betray'd indeed.

Adzounds, said Forster, never fear,
For the Brunswick army is not near ;
If they should come, our valour we'll show,
We will give them the total overthrow.

The lord Derwentwater then he found,
That Forster drawed his left wing round ;
I wish I was with my dear wife,
For now I do fear I shall lose my life.

Mackintosh he shook his head,
To see his soldiers there lye dead :
It is not so much for the loss of those,
But I fear we are all took by our foes.

Mackintosh was a valiant soldier,
He carried his musket on his shoulder :
Cock your pistols, draw your rapier,
And damn you, Forster, for you are a traytor.

The lord Derwentwater to Forster did say,
Thou hast prov'd our ruin this very day ;
Thou hast promised to stand our friend,
But thou hast prcved a rogue in the end.

The lord Derwentwater to Litchfield did ride,
In his coach and attendance by his side ;
He swore if he dy'd by the point of a sword,
He'd drink a health to the man he lov'd.

Thou Forster has brought us from our own home,
Leaving our estates for others to come ;
Thou treacherous rogue, thou hast us betrayed :
We are all ruin'd, lord Derwentwater said.

The lord Derwentwater he was condemned,
And near unto his latter end,
And then his lady she did cry,
My dear Derwentwater he must die.

The Lord Derwentwater he is dead,
And from his body they took his head ;
But Mackintosh and some others are fled,
Who'd set the hat on another mans head.

THE COLLIERS RANT.

AS me and my marrow was ganning to wark,
We met with the devil, it was in the dark ;
I up with my pick, it being in the neit,
I knock'd off his horns, likewise his club feet.
 Follow the horses, Johnny my lad oh !
 Follow them through, my canny lad oh !
 Follow the horses, Johnny my lad oh !
 O lad ly away, canny lad oh !

As me and my marrow was putting the tram,
The low it went out, and my marrow went wrang,
You would have laugh'd had you seen the gam,
The deil gat my marrow, but I gat the tram.
 Follow the horses, &c.

Oh ! marrow, oh ! marrow, what dost thou think?
I've broken my bottle, and spilt a' my drink ;
I lost a' my shin-splints among the great stanes,
Draw me t' the shaft, it's time to gane hame.
 Follow the horses, &c.

Oh ! marrow, oh ! marrow, where hast thou been?
Driving the drift from the low seam,
Driving the drift, &c.
Had up the low, lad, deil stop out thy een !
    Follow the horses, &c.

Oh ! marrow, oh ! marrow, this is wor pay week.
We'll get penny loaves and drink to wor beek ;
And we'll fill up our bumper, and round it shall go,
Follow the horses, Johnny lad oh !
    Follow the horses, &c.

There is my horse, and there is my tram ;
Twee horns full of grease will make her to gang !
There is my hoggers, likewise my half shoon,
And smash my heart, marrow, my putting's a'
    done.
        Follow the horses, Johnny my lad oh !
        Follow them through, my canny lad oh !
        Follow the horses, Johnny my lad oh !
        Oh ! lad ly away, canny lad oh !

SONG XIV.

Weel may the Keel Row.

AS I went up Sandgate, up Sandgate, up Sand-
    gate,
As I went up Sandgate, I heard a lassie sing,
Weel may the keel row, the keel row, the keel
    row,
Weel may the keel row, that my laddie's in.

He wears a blue bonnet, blue bonnet, blue bonnet,
He wears a blue bonnet, a dimple in his chin ;
And weel may the keel row, the keel row, the
    keel row,
And weel may the keel row, that my laddie's in.

SONG XV.

Bonny Keel Laddie.

MY bonny keel-laddie, my canny keel laddie,
My bonny keel-laddie for me O !
He sits in his keel as black as the deel,
And he brings the white money to me O.

SONG XVI.

NEWCASTLE BEER.

BY MR. JOHN CUNNINGHAM.

WHEN Fame brought the news of Great Britain's
  success,
  And told at Olympus each Gallic defeat ;
Glad Mars sent by Mercury orders express,
  To summon the deities all to a treat :
      Blithe Comus was plac'd
      To guide the gay feast,
And freely declar'd there was choice of good cheer ;
      Yet vow'd to his thinking,
      For exquisite drinking,
Their nectar was nothing to Newcastle beer.

The great god of war, to encourage the fun,
  And humour the taste of his whimsical guest,
Sent a message that moment to Moor's * for a tun
  Of stingo, the stoutest, the brightest and best ;
      No gods—they all swore,
      Regal'd so before,

---

* Moor's, at the sign of the Sun, Newcastle.

With liquor so lively, so potent, and clear :
  And each deified fellow
  Got jovially mellow,
In honour, brave boys, of our Newcastle beer.

Apollo perceiving his talents refine,
 Repents he drank Helicon water so long ;
He bow'd, being ask'd by the musical Nine,
 And gave the gay board an extempore song :
  But ere he began,
  He toss'd off his cann :
There's nought like good liquor the fancy to clear:
  Then sang with great merit,
  The flavour and spirit, .
His godship had found in our Newcastle beer.

'Twas stingo like this made Alcides so bold,
 It brac'd up his nerves and enliven'd his pow'rs;
And his mystical club, that did wonders of old,
 Was nothing, my lads, but such liquor as ours.
  The horrible crew
  That Hercules slew,
Were Poverty—Calumny—Trouble—and Fear :
  Such a club would you borrow,
  To drive away sorrow,
Apply for a jorum of Newcastle beer.

Ye youngsters, so diffident, languid, and pale,
 Whom love, like the cholic, so rudely infests ;
Take a cordial of this, 'twill *probatum* prevail,
 And drive the cur Cupid away from your breasts :

Dull whining despise,
Grow rosy and wise,
No longer the jest of good fellows appear ;
Bid adieu to your folly,
Get drunk and be jolly,
And smoke o'er a tankard of Newcastle beer.

Ye fanciful folk, for whom Physic prescribes,
Whom bolus and potion have harass'd to death !
Ye wretches, whom Law and her ill-loking tribes
Have hunted about 'till you're quite out of
breath !
Here's shelter and ease,
No craving for fees,
No danger,—no doctor,—no bailiff is near !
Your spirits this raises,
It cures your diseases,
There's freedom and health in our Newcastle beer.

Finis.

Mr. C. H. Stephenson has kindly supplied the following notes.

Notes to Yorkshire Garland.

YORKE, YORKE, FOR MY MONIE.

Page 103.—"His name is Maltbie."
Christopher Maltbie, draper, Lord Mayor 1583.

Page 104.—"The maior of Yorke."
Thomas Appleyard, Lord Mayor in 1584.

Notes to Northumberland Garland.

Page 139.—THE BATTLE OF OTTERBURN.

The following account of this battle is given by Camden in his "Britannia," p. 850:—"There happened this year, (1388) at Otterburn, in Northumberland, a stout engagement between the Scots and English:—victory three or four times changing sides, and at last fixing with the Scots; for Henry Piercy, (for his youthful forwardness, by-named Hotspur) who commanded the English, was himself taken prisoner, and lost 1500 of his men; and William Douglas, the Scots general, fell, with the greater part of his army; so that never was there a greater instance of the martial prowess of both nations." Sir John Froysart (who lived at that time) gives a full account of this battle, and says that it was Earl James Douglas who was the Scottish general. See Eachard, Rapin, &c.

Page 140.—"Laye at the New Castell."

The Scots, in this inroad, lay before Newcastle three days, where there was an almost continual skirmish. Sir Henry Percy, (with his brother, had come to Newcastle, on the intelligence of the Scots being abroad) in one of these skirmishes, lost his pennon or standard; and pledging himself to redeem it, followed the Scots to Otterburn, where the battle took place. See *Froysart's Chronicles.*

A FYTTE.

Page 147.—" The blodye harte in the Dowglas armes."

The armorial ensigns of Douglas were argent, a man's heart, gules, and on a chief azure three stars of the first.

Page 153.—THE HUNTING OF THE CHEVIAT.

Percy says this old ballad was written by one *Richard Sheale*, about the time of Henry VI., in whose reign several James's were kings of Scotland. *See his notes on this poem.*

Page 153.—"That wear chosen out of shyars thre."

Three districts in Northumberland, which still go by the name of *shires*, and are all in the neighbourhood of *Cheviot*. These are—*Islandshire*, so named from Holy Island ; *Norhamshire*, so called from the town and castle of Norham ; and *Bamboroughshire*, the ward or hundred belonging to Bamborough Castle.

Fit the Second.

Page 161.—" With his hart blood the wear wete."

This incident is taken from the battle of Otter-bourne, in which Sir Hugh Montgomery, Knight (son of John, Lord Montgomery), was slain with an arrow. See Crawford's *Peerage.*

Page 161.—" But even five and fifti."

The English were the first who took the field, and the last to quit it. They brought only 1500 to the battle, and the Scotch 2000. The English kept the field with fifty-three, the Scotch retiring with fifty-five.

Page 164.—" He dyde the battell of Hombyll-down."

The battle of Hombyll-down, or Humbledon, was fought September 14, 1402 (anno 3 Henry IV.), wherein the English, under the command of the Earl of Northumberland, and his son Hotspur, gained a complete victory over the Scots. The village of Humbledon is one mile north-west from Wooler in Northumberland. The battle was fought in a field below the village, near the present turnpike road, in a spot called *Battle-Riggs* or *Red-Riggs.* Humbledon is in Glendale Ward, a district so named in this county, and mentioned above in verse 63.

Page 165.—THE HUNTING IN CHEVY-CHASE.

This favourite old ballad is founded on the battle of Otterburn, as there never was a Percy engaged with a Douglas, but at that time ; though the Percy, who commanded at that battle, was not Earl of Northumberland, yet he was heir to that title, though he did not live to enjoy it.   Ben Johnson used to say he had rather have been the author of this ballad than of all his works.   In the *Discourse of Poetry*, Sir Philip Sidney speaks of it in the following words :—" I never heard the old song of Piercy and Douglas, that I found not heart more moved than with a trumpet ; and yet it is sung by some blind croudes, with no rougher voice than rude style ; which being so evil apparelled in the dust and cobweb of that uncivil age, what would it work trimmed in the gorgeous eloquence of Pindar?"   Addison eulogizes it highly in Nos. 70 and 74 of *The Spectator.*   And in the second volume of Dryden's *Miscellanies*, there may be found a translation of "Chevy Chase" into Latin rhymes by Henry Bold, of New College.

Page 165.—"The child may rue that is unborn."

The way of considering the misfortune which this battle would bring upon posterity . . . . is wonderfully beautiful and conformable to the way of thinking among the ancient poets.—ADDISON.

Page 171.—" The dead man by the hand."
Addison praises this line as wonderfully beautiful and pathetic.

THE MIDFORD GALLOWAY'S RAMBLE.

Page 194.—" But for to make short a long
story." My copy reads—"But just to make short
of the story."

Page 194.—" It scamper'd on northward away."
My copy reads—" It scamper'd right northward
away.

Page 197.—*Hedlowood* = Hedleywood.
   Cocket = Coquet.

Page 198.—*Thranton-bred* = Thrunton.
   Leirchil = Learchid.
   Lemendon, Allerwick = Lemington,
   Abberwick.

Page 199.—*Beenly* = Beanly.
   Galloway = Callaly.

At Callaly, the seat of the Claverings, tradition
reports that while the workmen were engaged in
erecting the castle upon a hill, a little distance
from the site of the present edifice, they were
surprised every morning to find their former day's
work destroyed, and the whole impeded by super-
natural obstacles, which causing them to watch,
they heard a voice saying :—

Callaly castle stands on a height
I'ts up in the day, and down at night ;

Build it down on the Shepherd's Shaw,
There it will stand and never fa'.

Upon which the building was transferred to the place mentioned, where it now stands.—*Northern Bards,* 1822.

Page 199.—*Ingrom, and Revely*=Ingram and Reavely.

Crowly=Crawley.

Culdmartin=Coldmartin.

Page 200. — *Wopperton*=Wooperton.

Rosdon=Rosedon.

THE HARE SKIN.

Note on line seven.

"A *gentleman* (Mr. Peter Consett) who loved pastime."

THE INSIPIDS.

Page 208.—"As sarey ald Sawney." My copy reads—"As sare as auld Sawney."

FELTON GARLAND.

Page 209.—*Jen—y Gow—n*=Jenny Gowen.

Page 210.—*Pet—r*= Peter.

THE LAIDLEY WORM.

Page 217.—"And not, till childy Wynd comes back." My copy reads—"And not, till Childly Wynd come back."

Page 218.—"The child of Wynd." My copy reads—"The child de Wynd."

Page 220.—"To sink the ship she went away." My copy reads—"To sink the ship she sent away."

ON THE FIRST REBELLION.

Page 224.—"With a jovial crew." Mackintosh's battalion consisted of thirteen companies of fifty men each.

Page 224.—"Adzounds, said Forster." Thomas Forster, jun., of Etherston, near Belford, in Northumberland, member of Parliament of the said county, was made general of the Pretenders army ; he was taken prisoner at Preston, but afterwards escaped out of Newgate, 1716.

Page 226.—"The Lord Derwentwater he is dead." James Radclyffe, Earl of Derwentwater, was beheaded on Tower Hill, 24th Febrruary 1715-16.

THE COLLIER'S RANT.

Page 228.—"Had up the lowe, lad;" *i.e.*, "Hold up the light."

WEEL MAY THE KEEL ROW.

The first verse in my version runs thus :—

As I cam' thro' Sandgate, thro' Sandgate, thro' Sandgate,

As I cam' thro' Sandgate, &c.

BONNY KEEL LADDIE.

The 2nd verse runs thus :—

Ha' ye seen owt o' my canny man,
  An' are ye shure he's weel O ?
He's geane o'er land wiv a stick in his hand,
  T' help to moor the keel O.

3rd verse.
The canny keel laddie, the bonny keel laddie,
  The canny keel laddie for me O ;
He sits in his huddock, and claws his bare
    buttock
  And brings the white money to me O.

THE

North-Country

CHORISTER;

AN

UNPARALLED VARIETY

OF

EXCELLENT SONGS.

Collected and published together, for
general Amusement,

BY

A BISHOPRICK BALLAD SINGER. .

To drink good ale to clear my throat,
To hear the bagpipes spritely note,
To ramble round the North Country,
This is the life that pleaseth me.

DURHAM:

PRINTED BY L. PENNINGTON, BOOKSELLER.

MDCCCII.

Licensed and entered according to order.

CONTENTS.

I. Tommy Linn 247
II. Randal a Barnaby 249
III. The Joyful Maid and Sorrowful Wife 253
IV. The New Highland Lad . . 256
V. Laddy lye near me 258
VI. The Bonny Scot made a Gentleman . 259

THE NORTH-COUNTRY CHORISTER.

SONG I.

TOMMY LINN.

TOMMY LINN is a Scotchman born,
His head is bald, and his beard is shorn ;
He has a cap made of a hare skin ;
An elder man is Tommy Linn.

Tommy Linn has no boots to put on,
But two calves skins, and the hair it was on ;
They are open at the side and the water goes in :
Unwholesome boots, says Tommy Linn.

Tommy Linn has a mare of the gray,
Lam'd of all four, as I hear say ;
It has the farcy all over the skin :
It's a running yade, says Tommy Linn.

Tommy Linn no bridle had to put on,
But two mouses tails, and them he put on ;
Tommy Linn had no saddle to put on,
But two urchin skins, and them he put on.

Tommy Linn went to yonder hall,
Went hipping and skipping among them all ;
They ask'd what made him come so boldly in,
I'm come a wooing, says Tommy Linn.

Tommy Linn went to the church to be wed,
The bride followed after, hanging down her head;
She hung down her cheeks, she hung down her
  chin ;
This is a gloomy quean, says Tommy Linn.

Tommy Linns daughter sat on the 'stair,'
Oh, dear father, gin I be not fair !
The stairs they broke, and she fell in :
You are fair enough now, says Tommy Linn.

Tommy Linns daughter sat on the ' brig,'
Oh, dear father, gin I be not trig !
The bridge it broke, and she fell in,
You are trig enough now, says Tommy Linn.

Tommy Linn, and his wife, and his wifes mother,
They all fell into the fire together ;
They that lay undermost got a hot skin :
We are not enough, says Tommy Linn.

Randal a Barnaby.

I am Randal a Barnabys youngest son,
My fathers lands ' to me are' come,
My brethren are all gone unto their own homes,
For they were all choaked with good ale-bones.
    And it's Randal a Barnaby by name was I,
    That loved good liquor courageously.

Of late we were in number seven,
But six they are pack'd to the joys of heaven,
Their names to you I will display,
And eke their lives most carefully.
                And Randal, &c.

Will, the eldest, he died at Dover,
Was six years drunk and never sober.
In Kent a town in the South country,
There died my brother Anthony.
                And Randal, &c.

Hard was his fortune which did behap,
That he was found drunk in a good ale-fat,
Robert he died on Salisbury plain,
By Sir John Barleycorn he was slain.

> And Randal, &c.

When he had been drunk a whole year for his part,
The good ale-spiggot struck him to the heart.
Richard he died at the Bath in the South,
With a pot in his hand and a pipe in his mouth.

> And Randal, &c.

When he had been drunk a whole year or more,
His throat, by chance, was cut by a whore.
Thomas he died in the Isle of Wight,
Was five years drunk both day and night.

> And Randal, &c.

For drinking and smoaking was the jolliest ad,
That ever old Randal a Barnaby had.
Leonard he dy'd on Wakefield green,
A whole year drunk and never was seen.

> And Randal, &c.

All good things he set by at nought,
For ale and tobacco was all his thought,
Ale and tobacco brought him to decay,
One dry'd him within, t'other wash'd him away.

> And Randal, &c.

My brethren are all dead and gone,
And I poor Randal am left alone,
As in a few days you shall understand,
I was made heir to my fathers land.

And Randal, &c.

PART II.

I courted a girl, and she was a dame,
And Margery Gaygood was her name ;
Her gentle old father gave unto me,
Twelve hundred pounds in gold and fee.

And Randal, &c.

Every month a hundred pound I laid,
Until my merry gold was all paid,
But where do you think I laid it up ?
Some in the cann and some in the cup.

And Randal, &c.

Before a whole year was come about,
Of all my money I left not a groat,
To borrow of my friends I ne'er would stand,
But pawn'd and mortgag'd all my land.

And Randal, &c.

I went to one master clean and round,
And he lent me two thousand pound,
I sold my lands and pawn'd my deeds,
And then I was cloathed in courtly weeds.

And Randal, &c.

But at Toss-pot-hall it was sold and gone,
I knew not where to make my moan,
For then I became so wondrous poor,
That forced I was to beg for more.
                         And Randal, &c.

Then for a tinker I did seek,
To carry a budget for three-pence a week,
And while he was peeping into an old pan,
Away with his budget and tools I ran.
                         And Randal, &c.

Then I did meet a pedlar trim,
And soon I was hir'd to go with him,
And so I became a pedlars boy,
Until I stole his pack away.
                         And Randal, &c.

All men said it became me well,
And Robin Hood's pennyworths I did sell,
At Winchester town I happen'd at last,
And good ale I drank full fast.
                         And Randal, &c.

The pot and the glass on the table stood,
I look'd upon it and thought it good,
And as I was sitting the fire by,
I fell out of my chair, and there did die.
     And Randal a Barnaby by name was I,
     That loved good liquor courageously.

SONG III.

[THE JOYFUL MAID AND SORROWFUL WIFE.]

MY gown was of the London black,
　Many a yard about ;
My petticoat of the scarlet red,
　And laced unto my foot.
　　And then I was a maid, a maid,
　　And joy came to me then ;
　　Of meat and drink, and rich cloathing,
　　I'm sure I wanted none.

My stockings was of the primrose coour,
　The half of them was silk,
My shoes was of the Spanish leather,
　My buckles was of gilt.
　　　　　　　　And then, &c.

My smock was of the white linen,
　As white as the driven snow ;
The belt that was about my middle,
　Was silk and silver O.
　　　　　　　　And then, &c.

The beads hang black about my neck,
    And many a ring within;
The blue lawn that was on my head,
    Was well worth ten shillings.
                        And then, &c.

There came a young man to my bed side,
    And asked me if I would wed;
He was so full of courtesy,
    I agreed to what he said.
        And then was I a wife, a wife,
            And sorrow came to me then;
            Of care and strife, and weary life;
            I'm sure I wanted none.

My gown was of the London black,
    And never a yard about;
My petticoat of the russet grey,
    And rags unto my foot.
                        And then, &c.

My stockings of the primrose colour,
    And clouted round about;
My shoes was of the Spanish leather,
    The bottoms of them was out.
                        And then, &c.

My smock was of the unbleach'd 'yarn,'
    And many a hole within,
The belt that was about my middle
    Was a good leather string.
                        And then, &c.

The beads hang black about my neck,
And never a ring within,
The blue lawn [that was] on my head,
Was scarce worth one farthing.
And then I was a wife, a wife,
And sorrow came to me then ;
Of care and strife, and weary life,
I'm sure I wanted none.

The New Highland Lad.

THERE was a Highland laddie courted a lawland
 lass,
There was, &c.
He promis'd for to marry her, but he did not tell
 her when ;
And 'twas all in her heart she lov'd her Highland
 man.

Oh where, and oh where does your Highland
 laddie dwell ?
Oh where, &c.
He lives in merry Scotland, at the sign of the
 Blue Bell ;
And I vow in my heart I love my laddie well.

What cloaths, O what cloaths does your Highland
 laddie wear ?
What cloaths, &c.
His coat is of a Saxon green, his waistcoat of the
 plaid ;
And it's all in my heart I love my Highland lad.

Oh where and oh where is your Highland laddie
gone ?
Oh where, &c.
He's gone to fight the [faithless] French whilst
George is on the throne,
And I vow in my heart I do wish him safe at
home.
And if my Highland laddie should chance to come
no more,
And if, &c.
They'll call my child a love-begot, myself a
common whore;
And I vow in my heart I do wish him safe on
shore.
And if my Highland laddie should chance for to
dye,
And if, &c.
The bagpipes shall play over him, I'll lay me
down and cry,
And I vow in my heart I love my Highland boy.
And if my Highland laddie should chance to
come again,
And if, &c.
The parson he shall marry us, and the clerk shall
say amen ;
And I vow in my heart I love my Highland man.*

---

* This song has been lately introduced upon the
stage by Mrs. Jordan, who knew neither the *words*,
nor the *tune*.

LADDY LYE NEAR ME.

AS I walked over hills, dales and high mountains,
I heard a lad and a lass making acquaintance ;
Making acquaintance and singing so clearly,
Long have I lain alone, laddy, lye near me.
   Near me, near me, laddy, lye near me.
   Long, &c.

What if I lay thee down, lassy, my deary?
Cannot I rise again?   Laddy, lye near me,
   Near me, &c.

If I get thee with bairn, lassy, my deary ;
Cannot I nurse the same?   Laddy, lye near me.
   Near me, &c.

I'll never marry thee, lassy, my deary.
Do as thou will, said she ; laddy, lye near me.
   Near.me, &c.

What will thy parents say, lassy, my deary?
Never mind, let us play ; laddy, lye near me.
   Near me, &c.

The Bonny Scot made a Gentleman.

O Jockey, O Jockey, before you go away,
One word with you, I pray you stay;
How came you now so gallant and gay,
Thou went but a begging the other day?
    Bonny Scot, we all witness can,
    That England hath made thee a gentleman.

Thy blue bonnet, when thou came hither,
Could scarce keep out the wind and weather;
But now it is turn'd to a hat and a feather,
Thy bonnet is blown the devil knows whither.
    Bonny Scot, &c.

Thy shoes on thy feet when thou cam'st from
    plough,
Were made of the hide of an old Scots cow;
But now they are turn'd to a rare Spanish leather,
And deck't with roses altogether,
    Bonny Scot, &c.

Thy stockings they were made of a neat blue,
They scarce cost six-pence when they were new;
But now they are turn'd to another hew,
With silken garters down to thy shoe.
    Bonny Scot, &c.

Thy waistcoat and doublet they were but thin
Where many a great louse has harbour'd in ;
But now it is turn'd to a scarlet red,
With silver and gold lace all bespread.
　　　Bonny Scot, &c.

Thy shirt which thou used to wear on thy back,
Was made off the web of a coarse hop sack ;
But now it is turn'd to a rare Holland fine,
Bought with the rare [old] English coin.
　　　Bonny Scot, &c.

Thy bands and thy cuffs which thou us'd to wear,
Was scare wash'd three times in a whole year ;
But now they are turn'd to a cambrick clear,
And deck'd with lace up to the ear,
　　　Bonny Scot, &c.

Thy gloves they were made of a threaden stitch
Thou kept on thy hands to hide the itch ;
But now they are turn'd to kid leather, I'm told,
And trimmed about with ribbons of gold.
　　　Bonny Scot, &c.

Thy sword at thy arse was a great black blade
With a great basket hilt of iron made ;
But [now] a long rapier doth hang by his side,
And huffling doth this bonny Scot ride.
　　　Bonny Scot, we all witness can,
　　　That England hath made thee a gentleman

THE END.